The dark night enveloped them

"You're so soft," Julian murmured. "I dreamed of your softness—longed for it." His mouth moved hungrily from the base of her throat to seek the budding tips of her breasts.

"And you're so damned arrogant," Anne breathed helplessly as his tongue moved tantalizingly over one nipple.

"But I can make you shimmer in my arms, can't I?" he whispered tenderly.

"Only because...."

"Because?"

Anne sighed in surrender. She couldn't tell him that she loved him. Not yet.

THE AUTHOR

Jayne Ann Krentz lives in Seattle, Washington with her engineer husband Frank and a yellow parakeet named Ferd. This prolific author, whose pen names include Stephanie James and Jayne Castle, has written more than thirty books. Asserting she has no fascinating hobbies, Jayne confesses only to enjoying country and western music and sampling a fine glass of wine.

Books by Jayne Ann Krentz

HARLEQUIN TEMPTATION
11–UNEASY ALLIANCE
21–CALL IT DESTINY
34–GHOST OF A CHANCE

These books may be available at your local bookseller.

Don't miss any of our special offers. Write to us at the following address for information on our newest releases.

Harlequin Reader Service
P.O. Box 52040, Phoenix, AZ 85072-2040
Canadian address: P.O. Box 2800, Postal Station A,
5170 Yonge St., Willowdale, Ont. M2N 5T5

Ghost of a Chance

JAYNE ANN KRENTZ

Harlequin Books

TORONTO • NEW YORK • LONDON
AMSTERDAM • PARIS • SYDNEY • HAMBURG
STOCKHOLM • ATHENS • TOKYO • MILAN

Published November 1984

ISBN 0-373-25134-3

Printed in Canada

1

THERE WAS NO EASY WAY for a woman to start a conversation with the man who had once sworn he'd return to claim her. Not when the man had failed to keep his promise.

Ghosts of memories flitted through Anne Silver's mind as she raised her hand to knock on the cabin door. The ghosts were not only in her head tonight, she decided. They were howling in protest as they were blown about by the first bitter winds of approaching winter. The cold came early in these Colorado mountains. It was only the middle of October. Back home in Indiana folks were still enjoying a pleasantly crisp autumn. But here in the mountains the ghosts of the coming winter already heralded snow. With her luck, Anne thought, the storm would probably arrive tonight.

Perfect. Just perfect. She would have to contend with both the phantom of a love that had never had a chance to be born and the specter of snow. Life, Anne decided wryly, had never promised to be fair in its dealings. The only intelligent way to handle tonight's task was to treat the entire matter as strictly business.

But as soon as her small fist had struck the door she knew how utterly impossible that goal was. There was no way on earth she would ever be able to handle Julian Aries in a strictly business fashion. Not when her whole being burned with chaotic emotions just at the thought of seeing him again.

She had alternated between states of longing and

fury for too many months. There was no longer any room in her for logic and superficial politeness. As soon as that thought entered her head she tried to banish it. *I'm a thirty-one-year-old woman. I can handle the coming scene as a mature adult. I will not let him know that I waited and waited....*

There was no sound of movement from behind the heavy wooden walls of the cabin but quite suddenly the door swung inward. Anne experienced a childish, irrational desire to flee as she faced the man who stood in the doorway. But thirty-one years and an ingrained determination came to her aid.

"Good evening, Julian. It's been a long time. May I come in? It's getting cold out here."

"Anne."

She couldn't tell if her name was a statement or a curse. It was spoken in the soft, velvet growl she remembered so well, but there was an edge to it that sent a chill down her spine. She kept her chin high and her gaze unflinching as Julian's tawny eyes swept over her.

She recalled the dark golden gaze as clearly as she remembered the voice, but there was something different about it, too, this evening. Even in the pale gleam of the porch light she sensed that the gold burned with an unnatural brightness. It was her imagination, Anne told herself. It had been six months since she'd last seen him and she was overreacting now. A gust of chill wind gave her an excuse to break the tense moment.

"Julian? It's freezing out here."

He stepped back into the firelit room. "Sorry. You took me by surprise. You must realize you're just about the last person I expected to find at my door this evening." He turned away, moving toward the overstuffed chair on one side of the fireplace.

Anne stared in startled fascination as she saw the

limp that altered the flowing, catlike stride she remembered. "Julian, you've been hurt?"

"Sit down, Anne." The too-bright gaze willed her to the chair, and the soft voice contained the old element of command. "I'll pour you some brandy. I'm sure you could use it. And not just because of the cold."

Without a word she sat down across from him. The firelight flared briefly, illuminating one side of his rough-cast face. With a hunger she didn't want to acknowledge, she drank in the sight of him. The nose that looked as though it had once been broken, the heavily etched lines at the edges of his mouth, the cheekbones that gave him such a leonine look and the thick black brows that framed the tawny eyes. Everything about him was the same, yet everything was different. Anne felt another uneasy chill.

Then he leaned forward to pour the expensive brandy from a bottle beside his chair. For a moment his face was at a different angle in the firelight, and she saw the scar that ran along the edge of his jaw.

"Julian, you have been hurt," she whispered. "What happened?"

"Roughly what you predicted would happen," he retorted, handing her the balloon-shaped glass. The shadows concealed the scar again as he sank back into the depths of his chair and regarded her with his overbright eyes. "I can hardly take in the fact that you're here. The last time we saw each other you were yelling something about never wanting to see me again."

And you were swearing that you'd come back to find me because we had unfinished business, she countered silently. "Was I yelling at you?" she managed to ask almost calmly, determined to maintain her self-control at all costs. "I do remember I was trying very hard to get across a particular point."

He nodded, giving her a brief, unexpectedly savage smile. He looked his age tonight, Anne thought. She knew vaguely that sometime during the past year he had turned forty. With a touch of whimsy she wondered if he were an Aries by birth as well as by name. What had happened to him during these past six months? The man who sat across from her tonight was the same one who had left her, vowing to return, but there was a difference in him.

It was enough of a difference to make her both wary and oddly frightened. If only he wouldn't look at her so intently, as if she were prey. Those tawny eyes seemed more dangerous than the flames in the fireplace and that smile.... She'd never seen him smile in that brutal manner.

"You made your point six months ago, Anne. You wanted me out of your life."

"I was very upset at the time," Anne began carefully.

"You were hysterical," he corrected bluntly.

Some of the fury that had alternated with the unfulfilled longing inside her for the past several months flared briefly. "I was not hysterical. I was furiously angry. There's a distinct difference."

He poured more brandy for himself, his eyes never leaving her face. "All right, you were furiously angry. It was difficult at the time to tell the difference between anger and hysteria."

Anne's hands clenched into small fists in her lap as she struggled to retain control of herself. "I had a right to behave the way I did. What did you expect from me after what you'd done? I begged you not to take Michael with you on that last mission. Two weeks later you brought him home with a bullet in his chest. He spent a week in that hospital. You didn't even hang around long enough to find out if he would survive. You were gone by midnight the same day you brought him back!"

"Ah, yes. Your precious Michael. How is your brother, Anne?"

Anne blinked and drew in a deep breath. "Back in a hospital," she returned flatly.

There was a faint pause while Julian considered that news. "Problems from that six-month-old wound?"

"No. Problems from being hit by a car in downtown Boston. This time he very nearly did die."

Something flickered in the tawny eyes, perhaps a flash of genuine compassion. "I'm sorry, Anne. I didn't realize. He seems to lead an adventurous sort of life, doesn't he?"

"Almost as adventurous as your own. Unfortunately, he doesn't have quite as much luck as you seem to have."

"He'll live?"

"Yes, he'll live."

Julian's gaze narrowed thoughtfully. "Why is it that instead of playing the loving sister by his bedside, you're wandering around these mountains at ten o'clock at night looking for me? Have you come to hurl accusations again? Going to find a way to prove that I was responsible for Michael being hit by a car the way you decided I was responsible for him being shot six months ago?"

Anne shook her head, trying to find the words. "It wasn't your fault."

The overly bright gaze hardened. The brief flicker of compassion was gone as if it had never existed. "How very magnanimous of you."

"Julian, please, I haven't come here to argue."

"Then why have you come? I'll admit that I'm a little curious on that score. Actually, there are a number of questions that come to mind. Why don't we begin at the beginning? How did you find me?"

"Michael had your last letter in his files. The one you sent from Denver telling him you were going to take some time off and spend it at your cabin in the mountains. You invited him here to go trout fishing. There was a small map at the bottom of the letter."

"I was feeling a bit lonely at the time," Julian remarked dryly. "I've since recovered."

"From the loneliness? Or from your 'accident'?" Anne demanded gently. "Julian, what happened to you?"

"Nothing you need worry about. In any event, we're still working on my questions. So you found out where I was from that letter I wrote in a moment of sentimental weakness. That doesn't tell me what you're doing here. Or why you're not at your brother's bedside."

"Michael's fiancée is at his bedside," Anne told him stiffly.

"Lucky Michael. He never seems to lack for angels of mercy to soothe his fevered brow."

Anne ignored the cynical inflection in his voice, frowning as he swallowed another large sip of brandy. He appeared to have made severe inroads into the bottle this evening before she had arrived, and he wasn't slowing down now. "Lucy and Michael met about three months ago. They're planning on being married around Thanksgiving." Anne hesitated and then asked anxiously, "Julian, don't you think you've had enough brandy?"

He stared at her over the rim of the glass, and Anne instantly regretted the impulsive words. There was a strangeness in the laconic, derisive expression that shaped his hard face; some element she didn't recognize. Julian had changed. Or was it simply that she'd never had a chance to really get to know him six months ago? A restless wariness made her shift slightly in her chair. Seeking something to do with her hands she rearranged the red, brass-buttoned jacket she had worn over her jeans and sweater. The coat was lying across the arm of her chair because Julian had not offered to hang it up for her.

"Enough brandy," he repeated. "Is it possible to have too much, do you think?" He sounded as though he had uncovered an interesting philosophical question.

"Yes, it's possible," she shot back firmly. "Highly probable, in your case, I'd say. Julian, you're acting very strangely tonight. I think it's probably because you've had too much to drink."

"You're wrong. It's not because of the brandy that I seem a bit, umm, disoriented. It's because I opened my door a few minutes ago and found you standing there. A severe shock to the system, I assure you."

"You were always fairly adept at dealing with the unexpected."

"Perhaps I'm slowing down in my old age. I'm forty now. Did you know that?"

"I remembered. Six months ago you told me that forty was a good age at which to consider a career change."

"I may have miscalculated." He poured some more brandy.

It seemed to Anne that the glass in his hand trembled slightly and that Julian took great care setting down the bottle. Too much care for a man whom she recalled as having a lithe, assured grace. That masculine grace had seemed second nature in him six months ago. Was he drunk or had he changed in that respect, too? She had known tonight's meeting would be difficult, but she hadn't expected to find herself confronting a man who looked at her with a devil's hot eyes.

"Have I really upset you so much by showing up like this?" Anne asked quietly.

"How would you feel if someone you'd seen far too much of in dreams suddenly walked into your life?" His mouth twisted wryly.

Anne barely caught herself in time to keep from telling him that she knew exactly how it felt. He had haunted her dreams for the past six months. The possibility that she had also been featured in his gave her a cautious flare of hope.

"Did you dream about me, Julian?"

"Dreams. Nightmares. Hard to tell the difference."

"Nightmares!" She felt crushed.

"How did you think I'd remember you? As a loving, generous woman? Not likely. What was it you said to me the night I asked you to go to bed with me? Something along the classic lines of 'not if you were the last man on earth,' I believe. No, you haven't figured in my dreams as a warm and tender memory, Anne. Every time I've seen you, awake or asleep, you've been telling me exactly what you thought of me. It wasn't very flattering."

The anger she had tried to bury blazed to the surface once more. "You've got a hell of a nerve being bitter, Julian Aries. I'm the one who has a right to be feeling resentful!"

"Resentful. What a bland word. Go ahead and feel resentful, Anne. It's nothing compared to how I feel." Julian leaned forward, cradling the brandy glass in his hands as he pinned her beneath a molten glare. "Want to know what I've felt during the past few months? I've felt like tracking you down and taking you away to someplace nice and secluded. Someplace like this cabin for example. I've felt like stripping you naked and laying you down on that rug in front of the hearth. I've felt like crushing you beneath me until you had no choice but to wrap your arms around me. I've felt like taking you again and again until you couldn't do anything else except respond, until you could no longer hurl recriminations or accusations, until you could no longer even think, until you could only plead with me to stop and then plead with me to do it all over again. And do you know what I was going to do then?"

Anne was shaking; a fine, almost undetectable physical reaction that was similar to shock. There was no love or even real desire in his words. Each phrase was coated in icy lightning. She knew exactly how his fantasy would end. "When you had me broken and begging beneath you, you would laugh at me, remind me of how I had once told you I'd never let you make love to me and then you'd walk away. I have a fairly vivid imagination, Julian. You don't need to spell it out. I just hadn't realized how much you hate me." She leaned her head back against the chair, closing her eyes wearily. "Coming here tonight was a mistake. I can see that now."

He didn't move. "Why are you here, Anne?"

"It doesn't matter. I should never have appeared on your doorstep like this." It was going to be a long drive back to the nearest mountain town and a hotel. A very long drive. And she was so tired. She'd been on her feet for almost forty-eight hours. There had only been that brief nap in the airplane on the flight to Denver. The thought of having an excuse to see Julian again as well as the urgency of her errand had kept her going. But this strange man with the golden eyes was killing her delicate fantasy and all the hope that had nourished it. She had been a fool.

"Why are you here, damn it? Answer me."

Anne opened her eyes and instinctively tried to retreat farther back into the depths of the chair. He hated her, she realized wildly. This wasn't the same, totally controlled man who had left her six months ago. The firelight gleamed on the jet-black hair that was marked with shafts of slate gray, the flames were reflected in his eyes and the set line of his mouth promised no gentleness or mercy.

"I'll go," she promised, shaken. Awkwardly she tried to scramble from the chair. He stopped her with a hand on her arm. Even through the fabric of her sweater she could feel the heat in his grasp. She could also feel the strength in him. Whatever had happened to him during the past six months, it hadn't diminished the power in his hands.

"You're not going anywhere," he rasped softly. "It was your decision to walk into the lion's den and now you'll have to live with it. In case you didn't hear it, the gate's already locked behind you."

Her eyes widened as she sat tensely chained in his grasp. "What are you talking about?"

"If it isn't snowing out there by now, it soon will be. You'd need chains to get down off this mountain tonight...if I were inclined to let you go, which I'm not."

"Julian, I can see this was all a mistake...."

"Not the first one you've made. But maybe the first one for which you'll actually have to pay. Why did you come, Anne?"

She caught her breath. "To ask for your help." Under the lash of the command in his voice, the words were out before she could halt them. To her surprise, they appeared to startle him.

"My help!" He released her and sat back. Above the rim of his glass he regarded her with puzzlement. "You came all this way to ask me for help?" He sounded incredulous.

Anne sat very still, afraid to provoke another show of physical strength. Against it she was helpless. Her only hope now lay in controlling the tense, highly charged situation she had created. "I don't know too many people with your particular qualifications, Julian. When Michael was nearly killed, Lucy and I knew we had to do something. I found his notes and his plans when I went through his desk. I decided to go ahead with his scheme but I'll need help.''

He shook his head once, as if she were annoying him. "You're not making any sense."

"I'm sorry, I'm a little nervous."

"I always did have that degree of power over you, didn't I? Six months ago I made you nervous, too." He smiled bitterly. "Maybe if I put my mind to it, I could really terrorize you."

"Stop it, Julian," Anne snapped. "Why are you acting like this? Because I refused your offer of a one-night stand six months ago? Come off it. Somewhere along the line you must have learned to handle a few minor rejections."

"You'll have to forgive me," he growled caustically. "Perhaps I'm not quite as forbearing as I once was. It's been a rough six months, lady. Let's skip the recriminations and get on to the business end of this meeting. You are here on business, I assume?"

Anne nodded cautiously. "I need your help, Julian."

"How badly?" He cocked a heavy, dark brow.

"I beg your pardon?"

"Forget it. We'll get to that part later. Why do you need my help?"

Anne touched the tip of her tongue to her lower lip in a small gesture of anxiety. Her fingers twisted in her lap. "Because of my brother."

Julian eyed her intently. "Michael's in trouble?"

"They nearly killed him, Julian."

"Who's 'they'?"

"The people who ran him over. The accident was labeled hit and run by the police. No description of the car. No witnesses. Michael can only remember vaguely that the car was dark blue."

"As a professional journalist I thought he had

trained himself to make more accurate observations in the field," Julian said dryly.

"He nearly died. Under those circumstances it's tough to make accurate observations."

"He did a good job of it when I took him with me on that last mission. Even with a bullet in him he was busy making notes in a tape recorder until the moment he actually passed out."

Anne glanced away, concentrating on the fire. "He's a professional. That's something I didn't fully appreciate six months ago. I do now. He'll do whatever has to be done to get a story."

"What's this?" Julian mocked. "Are you actually telling me you realize it was his own decision to accompany me on that mission to the island? Does this mean I'm no longer the big bad wolf who lured him into danger and then got him shot?"

Anne's head swung around, her loosely coiled and knotted hair unraveling a little with the abrupt movement. "You approached him first. You needed him for cover, remember? You were going to play photographer and he was supposed to be the writing part of the team. His credentials were solid and you knew he wouldn't be questioned. As his photographer you could ride on those credentials."

"Aha! So I haven't been miraculously exonerated. I'm still the fast-talking agent who convinced him to risk his life for a story just so I could use him for a shield." Julian nodded judiciously, as if satisfied with his analysis.

Fast-talking agent, Anne echoed silently. Yes, Julian had been fast talking. Also fast moving and lethally swift at everything else he did. He had wanted her from the moment he'd met her and had made no secret of that fact. In the whirlwind week of planning and preparation that had preceded the mission, Julian had used every spare moment to break down her defenses. Anne knew she had been unable to conceal the desire he aroused in her, but she had managed to stop herself from surrendering completely.

"I told you I didn't come here to get involved in that old argument. It was over six months ago."

"Not for me, it wasn't. I had to go back to that island. With memories of you standing in the hospital corridor outside Mike's room telling me you never wanted to see me again and blaming me for the bullet in Mike's chest. Remember that little scene, Anne? It's very firmly etched in my mind. I've had a lot of time to think about it. So dramatic, with you slapping my face the way you did in front of the head nurse and her staff."

"You handled the whole thing with your customary self-control. You didn't even slap me back." She remembered that scene. Because in addition to blaming him for bringing her brother back wounded, she'd wanted to plead with him not to return and finish the mission. She would have gotten down on her knees and begged but she had known at the time that it was hopeless. Nothing she could have said or done would have altered his decision to complete the job. Julian had been assigned, by the vague government agency for which he worked, to gain intelligence information on a terrorist ring based on a remote island in the Caribbean. He was a professional. Anne had known that she was helpless to keep him from going back and risking his life. That sense of helpless frustration had fueled her fury that night in the hospital corridor.

"I thought later that perhaps I should have," Julian mused.

"Slapped me? That was never your way, Julian. You're the icy, controlled, macho type, remember? You let me throw a tearful, screaming tantrum in the hospital corridor and then you just walked away." *Promising you'd be back*, she concluded silently. *Only you never came back to me, Julian.*

"I hadn't realized I'd left such an indelible impression on you," he grated, helping himself to more brandy. "It's getting hot in here," he added in abrupt irritation. He opened the collar of the black, long-sleeved flannel shirt he wore with his jeans. "I should douse that fire."

"Maybe you've had a little too much of that brandy," Anne ventured as an explanation.

Julian sighed. "If it's the brandy that's making me feel so warm, I'll just have to suffer. I need the alcohol more than I need a change of temperature." He lowered his lashes, concealing the heat in his eyes. "Let's see if we can get this conversation back on whatever track it was trying to follow. You're here. Presumably because you need something, not because you were curious about whether or not I ever got back from that damned island. Tell me again about the car that hit your brother."

Anne wanted desperately to go on talking about each other, but the rational side of her nature warned against the danger. She had to take this slowly.

"Michael was working on a project at the time he was hit by the car. He was investigating a strange theft ring that operates in a very unique fashion. The people in the ring pose as...as psychic phenomena investigators."

"Which means?"

"Ghost hunters."

"A time-honored profession," Julian observed wryly. "Why was Mike bothering to uncover a few more false psychic types? Houdini exposed dozens, and all it did was increase the general interest in mediums and other fakes."

"I told you, it's a theft ring. These people pose as psychic investigators to gain access to beautiful old homes that are filled with valuable antiques and paintings and just plain cash. They prey on the gullibility of eccentric little old ladies who believe they actually have haunted houses, as well as on a certain, trendy type who decides it's chic to have a resident ghost in the family mansion. The ghost-hunting exercises make for unusual weekend parties for the owner and his friends, I gather. Once inside the house, the ring goes through its little rituals to exorcise the ghost. Séances, confrontations with the ghost, that sort of nonsense."

"Meanwhile they're casing the house? Making wax impressions of keys? Learning the ropes of whatever security system might be installed?"

"Exactly. Michael was fascinated. He's always had a secret interest in ghosts and psychic phenomena. He's done a few articles on the subject in the past. Just for fun, I suppose. At any rate, he made a lot of contacts during the year he researched the stuff. A few months ago he started hearing rumors about a particularly successful band of ghost hunters and his old curiosity was aroused."

"If everyone knows the ghost hunters are really stealing from the houses they're supposed to, uh, deghost, why don't the police take care of them?" Julian moved a little restlessly, unbuttoning another button on his black shirt. His gaze went to the fireplace. Outside, the wind began to howl more loudly.

Anne's uneasiness increased. Things were difficult enough as it was, trying to deal with a man who obviously felt nothing but hostility toward her. It seemed to her that she didn't need the added unpleasantness of a major snowstorm.

"No one does know the ghost hunters are carrying out the thefts," she explained. "It's a theory Michael has, based on the fact that some very valuable jewelry and other objects have since been reported missing at most of the houses that have employed the psychic investigators. The thefts aren't being discovered for months in some cases because, often, fakes have been substituted for the valuables. Paste jewelry, painting reproductions, that kind of thing. Michael hadn't discussed his theories with anyone because he wanted to break the story himself."

"And now he's back in a hospital for his trouble. You're sure there's a connection?"

"Between Michael's investigations and the fact that he was a victim of hit and run? Yes, I'm sure of it."

"Damn, it's hot in here." Uncoiling like a cat from the chair, Julian got to his feet and stalked to the front door. The impression of a cat was marred slightly by the limp. A wounded cat, Anne thought. Few animals were more dangerous. She watched uncomprehendingly as he flung open the door.

Instantly the noisy gale swept into the room, bringing the first snowflakes and a blast of freezing cold.

"Julian, what's wrong?"

He slammed the door shut after inhaling deeply a few times. "I told you, it's hot in here." He threw himself back into the chair and stared at her broodingly. "Does Michael know you're here?"

"No."

"But his fiancée does?"

Anne nodded. "Lucy and I decided something had to be done. It's obvious the police aren't going to pursue the hit and run. They have no evidence or descriptions to go on. Michael had a plan. I'm going to implement it."

"You're going to implement it?" he scoffed tightly.

"With your help," she added determinedly.

"My help," he repeated, shaking his head wonderingly. Firelight glinted on the dark depths of his hair and illuminated the slate gray buried there. "What makes you think I'd help you?"

Anne's jaw tightened but she kept her voice steady. "I understand that you wouldn't go out of your way to do anything for me. I'm hoping you'll do it for Michael's sake."

He watched her impassively for a moment and then a new fierceness permeated his expression. "No."

Anne flinched. Using Michael's name had been her last hope. If he wouldn't do it for her brother's sake then she had nothing else with which to bargain. "Won't you even listen to the plan? It might... it might intrigue you." She glanced unconsciously around the cabin, wondering how long he'd been cooped up here alone. Perhaps something that took him out of these mountains might be good for him. Whatever had happened to Julian during the past six months had changed him, and not for the better. She found herself wishing he wouldn't look at her with that too-hot gaze. It seemed to Anne that she could feel all his anger and disgust as it radiated at her through those golden eyes. She had been an idiot to think this idea was going to work. A rather desperate idiot.

"There isn't much that intrigues me these days, Anne," he told her coolly.

"Not even the thought of getting out of this cabin?" she demanded. His own restlessness seemed to be affecting her. She didn't feel the overheated atmosphere of the room as he apparently did, but she was vividly aware of another kind of tension. The anxiety of crushed hopes, a determination to go forward with her brother's plan, even without Julian's help, and the realization that she was trapped in this place with a man who was dangerously different from the Julian she remembered all contributed to her disquiet. Anne picked up her brandy glass and took a steadying sip.

"I like this cabin," Julian said dryly. "It's the closest thing to a home that I've got. I'm sorry if it depresses you, but then, no one invited you here."

Anger flared in Anne. Well, she'd tried. That was all she could do. Setting the brandy glass down on the table with a sharp snap, she rose and collected the red jacket from the arm of the chair. "You're right. This place does depress me. You depress me. I think I'll make a stab at getting out of these mountains before the snow makes the driving impossible."

He was on his feet before she could turn around, his powerful hand closing over her shoulder. With the instincts of a rabbit being confronted by a wolf, Anne went very still, not daring to move.

"For you the trip out is already impossible. You should never have come here, Anne."

"I know that now." Her voice was a faint whisper. She realized she was trembling beneath his hand. What a fool she had been.

Slowly, inevitably he pulled her around to face him. The golden eyes were lit with a devastating, unnaturally brilliant fire, and the same heat was being conducted through his hand where it grasped her shoulder.

"Once I asked you to spend the night with me," he rasped softly. "The night before Mike and I had to leave for that island."

"I remember." And she did. All too clearly. Her mind had been at war with her body that night. She had known he was wrong for her—known there was no hope of building any kind of permanent relationship with a man who made his living the way Julian Aries did. Her mind had won the battle. It had drawn on her sense of anger toward the man who was taking her younger brother into a potentially deadly situation. She had used that fury to fight her own undisciplined desire.

"I let you walk away that night. I would be a fool to let you walk away again, wouldn't I? Not when you've been haunting me for six months."

The heat in him was reaching out to engulf her. A

new kind of fear sizzled along her nerve endings. Something was wrong and she didn't understand it.

"Julian, are you all right?" she asked again, not knowing how to ask the real question.

"No, I'm not all right. You've played havoc with my mind, Anne Silver. You came and went in my head like a ghost, turning up whenever I needed you but always staying just out of reach. I wanted to catch you and chain you. I wanted to possess you—make it impossible for you to escape."

"You wanted to hurt me, punish me," she protested. "But, Julian, I don't deserve your anger. You didn't hate me when you left that night after bringing Michael back. You said we had unfinished business, but I didn't think you hated me. What's wrong? What happened? Why are you—"

"Be quiet, ghost lady. I'm going to exorcise you. I'm going to get you out of my head once and for all."

His strong hands locked behind her head, thumbs moving along the line of her jaw so that she was forced to lift her face for his kiss. Their gazes clashed and in that moment Anne knew her premonition had been correct. She was dealing with a Julian who was far different from the man who had walked away from her six months ago.

2

HER HAIR WAS THE COLOR of autumn leaves. Julian snarled his fingers in the thick stuff, tugging it free from the tortoiseshell clip that had anchored it. How he'd longed for the rich russet color of her hair in the middle of that endless green jungle.

He'd wished for the sweet, womanly scent of her when the thick smell of decomposing undergrowth had threatened to clog his nostrils. And at night he'd dreamed of having the soft fullness of her body next to his. The nights had been the worst. It was then that she had floated in his head, taunting him, always just out of reach.

Julian had never been quite certain why he had been so fascinated with Anne Silver. His business with Michael had accidentally brought him into contact with her. As soon as she had discovered why he was spending so much time with her brother, Anne had begun to fight him. She saw him as a threat and in the end she had been right. A week had been too short a time to override her fears.

But he had known she was intensely aware of him. Julian had tried to play on that undeniable attraction—tried to use it to break through the barriers she had erected against him. He had failed. Anne had resisted him steadfastly, backed by her fierce desire to protect her younger brother and by her own instinctive wariness of Julian himself.

Only in his head had he been able to touch her like this, thread his fingers through the enthralling russet hair. Her blue-green eyes had looked at him often enough in his dreams, at times filled with accusation, at other times warm with desire. It was when he saw those eyes filled with need for him that Julian knew for certain he was hallucinating. Those times were the most dangerous. In a way he had come to see that fantasy of desire as a warning that he was losing his grasp on reality. He had relied on it to let him know that he was near the edge. In real life, Anne would never look at him with such sensual invitation.

That knowledge had infuriated him but it had also saved his life on more than one occasion. It had forced him to think logically enough to save his own neck when he otherwise might have slipped too deeply into the quagmire of his fevered mind.

"If I hadn't been half out of my mind a lot of the time, you would have driven me crazy," he growled against her mouth. Such a soft expressive mouth. Her smile could be brilliant, full of laughter and feminine mischief. He'd tortured himself with thoughts of how many other men she had used that smile on during the past six months.

"Julian, wait—"

He crushed the protest back into her mouth and the action was a catalyst. It unlocked all the raging hunger, as well as the raging frustration and anger that had been simmering in him. Remembered pain, both physical and mental, crowded into his head, seeking to be assuaged at last.

She tasted as he had dreamed she would taste. Warm and damp and inviting. The trace of brandy in her mouth was a piquant spice, blending with the overwhelmingly sensual flavor. It was better than he had dreamed, Julian told himself fiercely. Far better.

He felt her tremble in his grasp, heard her soft moan, and a feeling of exultation swept over him. She was here in his arms and he could hardly believe it.

This time it wasn't an hallucination or a fevered dream. This time she was real and she couldn't escape. He wouldn't allow it. Not when he'd waited so long for this night.

As he drank from her mouth, trying to satisfy a thirst that only grew stronger, Julian allowed himself the luxury of touch. The problem with hallucinations and dreams was that a man could never enjoy the exquisite sense of touch. His fingers moved along the delicate shape of her ear and then traced the line of her cheek.

She was no great beauty, he tried to tell himself for the thousandth time. The lines of her face were not classic. Rather they were a little rounded, slightly softened. Just as the lines of her body were round and soft. A man looked at her and knew she was all woman, capable of gentleness and fire. When she loved she would wrap a man in both, Julian thought. When she was angry she could be as fierce as any she-cat. The one thing Anne could never be was remote and distant. That knowledge gave him power.

"I've wanted you for so long," he ground out, as he reluctantly freed her mouth to explore the line of her throat. "So long.... You should never have come here tonight, lady. You should have had enough sense to stay out of my lair."

"Julian, we must talk—"

The words were muffled against his shoulder and he ignored them, concentrating on the way she was responding. When he had dared allow himself the fantasy, it had been exactly like this. She would murmur the words of protest because he knew that intellectually she was afraid of him. But her body always trembled under his touch, just as it did tonight.

He could feel the desire in her now. It made her shiver slightly and press closer. Her palms were flat against his chest, fingers splayed as if she were uncertain whether to fight or cling. Julian gave her no option. He drew his hands down the length of her back, seeking the full curve of her enticing derriere.

His head was beginning to spin a little. Only natural, he decided grimly. Having a fantasy come to life was disorienting. Wanting her arms around him he freed her momentarily to grasp her wrists and pull them behind his neck.

"You're not going anywhere tonight," he told her thickly, "so you might as well give me what I need. Hold me, Anne. Hold me as if you'll never let go."

The blood sang savagely in his veins when she did as he demanded. Intoxicated now, Julian groaned and bent to lift her into his arms. He would take her into the bedroom, he thought. Away from the heat of the damn fireplace. Between the two of them they would generate more than enough warmth anyway.

"Julian, you aren't the only one who's had dreams."

The small confession gripped him for an instant. He came to a halt beside the quilted bed and gazed down at her face. She had closed her eyes against him and the moment. "If I've figured in your dreams, it could only have been as a devil. That's how you've always seen me, isn't it?"

"I've hardly seen you at all. A few times before you left for that island with Michael and then that night you brought him home."

"Tonight you'll find out if all your worst fears are true, won't you?" He dropped her down onto the bed, following heavily. "At least I look the part now, don't I?" he demanded as her hand came up to touch the scar on his jaw.

"Please tell me what happened," she begged.

Julian studied the depths of her sea-colored eyes. "The last thing I want from you tonight is pity. Save it for some other man who will be satisfied with that kind of response. I want the fire and the softness."

But he knew that deep down he didn't want to witness her reaction to the marks on the rest of his body. His hand swept out to find the lamp switch even as his mouth closed over Anne's again. It wasn't just that he didn't want the light. He also didn't need the extra heat from the lamp. It was already so hot, even here in the bedroom away from the fire.

Somehow the sudden darkness seemed to fracture the languid spell that had governed Anne since he had first kissed her in the living room. When his hand moved hungrily to the gentle curve of her breast she cried out softly. He felt the sudden resistance in her and groaned.

"Anne, no. Don't fight me. I've waited too long— needed you too badly. You came looking for me tonight and you'll have to take what you've found."

The tension in her radiated through his own body and fed his desire. So many nights of wanting and longing. He had thought he was hallucinating again this evening when he'd answered the knock on his door to find his ghost lady standing on the step. He'd half expected her to simply disappear. And then she had complained about the cold and asked to come inside. He didn't think ghosts felt the cold.

Julian was aware that his fingers were shaking a little as he determinedly tugged off the sweater Anne wore. The knowledge irritated him. He would not give in to the weaknesses of his own body. Not tonight when his whole being was intent on exorcising his very personal phantom.

"You don't feel like a phantom, though," he muttered as the sweater came free and he found the tips of her breasts. The fact that she was not wearing a bra pleased him. One less obstacle to overcome.

"I'm real, Julian. Please treat me as if I am," she whispered. "Don't punish me for your nightmares. I never meant to haunt you."

Her fingers laced into his hair, stroking down to his nape almost as though she were trying to soothe him. Julian told himself that he didn't want to be soothed and gentled. Deliberately he fought the impulse to halt the lovemaking and simply lay his head down on her breast and allow her to stroke him. Always in his dreams that had been a dangerous lure the ghost had used. Always she withdrew her gentle touch just as he accepted it.

But this time Anne was real, he reminded himself. Wonderingly he grazed his fingertips across one nipple. When he felt it grow taut and sensitized he growled his pleasure.

"I know this is real," he murmured, bending his head to taste the budding nipple. "And this...." He slid his palm down her stomach until he felt her quivering response. She knew he was going to probe further and her whole body was reacting with unbearable anticipation and tension. The sense of power in him skyrocketed. For once his ghost lady was under his control.

The spinning sensation in his head seemed to accelerate. A throbbing urgency was governing his body. The forces driving him tonight were too elemental to allow for a leisurely, carefully charted act of desire. Impatiently Julian fumbled in the darkness with the clasp of her jeans.

"Oh, Julian!"

He couldn't be sure if it was a cry of protest or resignation or desire. He only knew he liked the sound of his name on her lips. With a quick, stripping action he pulled the jeans down over her rounded hips, heedless of her fingers as she struggled to slow him.

"Please, Julian, I...oh, *please!*"

He had found the secret, warm place between her legs and she shuddered as he made the contact. Already he could feel her dampening at his touch. She wanted him. Whatever else she said tonight, she couldn't deny that she wanted him.

"Give me the words, ghost lady. Let me hear you say that you need me tonight as much as I need you," he ordered, tracing an erotic design on the most intimate spot on her body.

Convulsively her hands went around him, her nails adding small marks to the collection of scars on his back. "I told you. You aren't the only one who's had dreams, Julian. I've longed for you. You promised to come back and you never did. You *promised*."

He heard the accusation and the pain in her voice and couldn't understand either one. But there was no way on earth he could fail to understand the sensuous twisting of her body as she moved pleadingly against him. His ghost lady was coming very much alive beneath his hands.

When he pulled away to fumble rapidly with his own clothing Anne murmured a protest. His shirt and jeans landed in a careless heap on the floor alongside the soft leather boots he had been wearing, and then Julian turned back to pin his phantom to the bed.

"There were times when I would have sold my soul to have you where you are now," he grated. "I won't let you escape, now that I've got my hands on you."

In the dark shadows he saw her lips part as if she were about to contradict him. Julian sealed them with his own, simultaneously pushing himself between her legs. The softness of her thighs around him was all he had ever dreamed it would be. For a moment he held back, not yet certain whether to believe.

"Closer, Anne," he commanded huskily. "Cling to me until I know you're real."

"I keep telling you, Julian, I'm very, very real." She sighed into his mouth and her arms tightened, pulling him to her.

He sensed the surrender in her and gloried in it. Head whirling with the satisfaction of knowing she was giving herself to him at last, Julian rasped her name and drove himself heavily into the snug, hot velvet of her.

"Anne, oh, my God, Anne...!"

No fantasy this, Julian thought dazedly. He could feel the instinctive resistance of her body as it gradually accommodated itself to the fullness of his manhood. There was an exciting, tantalizing tingle of pain as her nails flexed on his shoulders. And the silky feel of her legs was exquisite captivity. Nothing in his life had ever been so overwhelmingly real.

Frantically he forced himself to find the pace that would allow Anne to stay with him as he sought the promised satisfaction. He realized dimly that he had to make it good for her. In his fantasies he had always promised himself he would make it right for Anne, hoping that the sensual gratification would be an inducement to make her stay with him.

"Julian, darling Julian. Love me. Please, please love me...."

He was aware of the new tension in her, felt the gentle telltale shiver that coursed through her, pulling him along in its wake and suddenly it wasn't just his head that was spinning. It was the whole world.

"Anne!"

The cry was torn from him as his body exploded. Blazing satisfaction surged in him, and he held the woman in his arms tighter than he'd ever held on to anything or anyone in his life.

And then there was silence. Nothing but too much warmth and too much silence. He should have put out the fire, Julian thought vaguely as he closed his eyes. It was too damn hot.

Anne realized slowly that the forceful grasp that had held her was slackening. She came out of the too-silent sensual aftermath to find Julian sprawled across her body, his head on the pillow beside her. Uncertainly she opened her eyes to meet his, not knowing what to expect. After the shattering finale to the lovemaking there had been no words, no soothing caresses, no soft murmurs. Only silence.

Silence and heat, she corrected, frowning a little as she realized just how warm Julian was. Unnaturally warm. The tawny eyes that had seemed abnormally bright were concealed behind the only soft feature of his face—his lashes.

He was asleep.

So much for worrying about what a woman said in a situation such as this, she told herself ruefully. It looked as if she was going to be spared the humiliation of acknowledging her surrender to the man who had insisted on it.

Tentatively Anne lifted a hand to push back a swath of dark hair that had fallen forward across Julian's forehead. When her fingers brushed his skin she felt the warmth there.

"Julian?"

There was no response. He was deeply asleep. Carefully Anne began untangling her legs from his. In the shadows she could only make out the harsh angles of his face but she ran a palm lightly down his smoothly muscled back. There, just below his shoulders, was the ridge in the surface of his skin. She thought she had felt it during the moments of frantic passion. Another scar, she wondered.

Dear God. Julian had been hurt and badly. A fierce anger welled up inside as she carefully explored the length of the scar. Anne was filled with a sudden hatred for whoever had inflicted the physical pain on her lover. She remembered the limp and her brow furrowed again. Perhaps no one had deliberately done this to him. He might have had an accident for all she knew. What was it he had said? Something about a rough six months.

As she pulled herself free of the weight of his body Anne became aware of the chill in the bedroom. The heat of the fire had not penetrated well in here, and apparently Julian had switched on no alternative source. Unless she counted the source of heat that was his own body. Lord, he was hot. Much too hot.

A curious lethargy in her limbs made it difficult to get to her feet. She felt as though Julian had just forced her to run a hundred miles with him. Every part of her remembered the feel of his passion and strength. It had all been more real than she would have expected. Having a dream merge with reality should have been a more ethereal experience, Anne told herself. Something warned her that Julian had left an impression on her that would never be confused with a dream. Already she was vividly aware of a soft soreness in her lower body. In making her reach the peak of satisfaction with him, Julian had not spared her.

Awkwardly Anne started to pull on her clothes and then realized what she wanted in that moment was a hot shower. She found the adjoining bathroom, turned on the shower and stood studying the few masculine items arranged around the sink while she waited for the water to warm.

Julian used only the essentials, she thought. There wasn't even any after-shave lotion, let alone any men's cologne. There was a small black comb but certainly no styling dryer for his hair. Unable to stifle an overriding interest in the man who lay sleeping in the other room, Anne opened the small mirrored medicine chest.

A toothbrush. A tube of toothpaste, which had been consistently squeezed from the middle rather than from the bottom, and a razor. One can of shav-

ing cream. Feeling guilty at the blatant snooping,
Anne was about to close the door of the cabinet when
she noticed the bottle of tablets on the top shelf. Aspirin, she decided. If Julian really did have a slight fever
she could give him some later. Hastily she shut the
cabinet and stepped into the shower.

By the time she began responding to the invigorating effects of the hot water, Anne also began to take
stock of her situation. In every fantasy she had ever
spun concerning a reunion with Julian Aries, matters
had always taken a different course from the one they
had pursued tonight. She had dreamed of long, quiet
talks while they finally got to know each other. She
had imagined herself explaining that she now understood that Julian hadn't "lured" her brother to that
island. Michael Silver had a reporter's instincts and a
willingness to go wherever he had to go in order to
get his story. The story Julian had offered him in ex-
change for providing journalistic cover had been too
good to turn down.

Anne had planned to make her apologies and explanations and then wait to see if Julian still had any
interest in pursuing the electric attraction that had
flared between them from the first moment they had
met. She had been prepared to accept the limitations
his career would put on any relationship they built.
Or at least she had told herself she was prepared to
accept those limits.

In return she had wanted some answers. He had
promised to come back for her and he had never kept
that promise. She had to know if the attraction he had
felt wasn't sufficient to make him tolerate her anger
and the demands he undoubtedly expected her to
make. For six months she had waited for him to make
the first move.

In the end she had been forced to come to him. The
result had been explosive but not at all illuminating

or constructive. Deep down she had known that
sooner or later physically, at least, she would surrender. It had been inevitable and she suspected that
something in her had recognized that from the start.

The problem was that the sensual coupling could
provide no real, long-term answers. It only served to
solidify the chains that bound her to Julian. And she
had no way of knowing if even that much had been
accomplished from Julian's point of view.

He had claimed he wanted to exorcise her from his
mind. Perhaps tonight was all he would ever need
from her.

Tugging on the jeans and sweater and her warm
socks, Anne finished dressing and padded back out
into the dark bedroom. Julian still lay in a sprawl
across the bed. The light from the bathroom shafted
across the solid, lean lines of his body, revealing the
angry scar across his shoulders and another forbidding line along the back of his thigh. Her heart turned
over at the thought of the pain those wounds must
have inflicted.

Even as she fought back the instinctive reaction, Julian moved slightly on the bed. There was a restless
abruptness to the movement that alarmed her. He
mumbled something and flung his hand out over the
pillow.

"Julian, what's wrong?" She hurried forward and
sat down on the edge of the bed, testing the warmth of
him with her palm. "My God, you're burning up!"

In the few minutes she had been in the shower, the
fever she had sensed in him had blossomed into a fire.
Alarmed by the intensity of it, she struggled to get
him under the bedclothes.

"Too hot," he muttered, pushing at her with his
hands. "Much too hot. Put out the fire."

"Hush, Julian. It's all right. I'll take care of you."

Eyes closed he turned his head in the direction of

her voice. "Ghost lady. Why are you here? It's dangerous...."

"I'm here to take care of you, Julian. Please let me." She managed to pull the sheet over him although his movements were becoming more disturbed. His strength was a problem. Even gripped with fever his hands retained a lot of their normal power. When he tried to rip aside the sheet she was helpless to keep it in place.

"Julian, try to lie still. I'm going to get something to cool you down."

He was far too warm. When a fever soared like this it ought to be broken in any way possible. Somewhere she remembered hearing that bit of first-aid advice. Anne stopped battling him for the sheet and went back into the bathroom. Opening the medicine cabinet, she reached for the bottle of tablets she had noted earlier. They weren't aspirin. Frowning, she read the unfamiliar chemical name on the label and noted that they were a prescription.

"Two tablets at onset of symptoms. One every four hours thereafter," she read, wondering if the fever was one of the symptoms for which the tablets had been prescribed. Carrying the bottle back into the bedroom, she tried to get a moment of rational attention from her patient.

"Julian, are these pills for your fever?"

"Damn pills. Won't take them anymore. Tired of being a weakling. Go away, ghost lady. Take the pills with you. I hate it when you see me like this."

His body was dry from the inner heat. She had to do something. Determinedly Anne ran a glass of water in the bathroom and came back to the bed. Firmly she cradled him with an arm around his broad shoulders and held the liquid to his lips.

"You're thirsty, Julian. You must be thirsty. Here, put this in your mouth and drink the water."

To her astonishment he obeyed, swallowing the tablet and most of the water. When she attempted to remove her arm, however, he protested angrily.

"Don't go. Not now. Too late now."

"I'll be right back, Julian," she soothed. "I'm going to get something to cool you down a little."

"You'll come back?"

"Yes."

"Can't trust you. You always fade away."

"Not this time, Julian. Not this time."

Desperate to relieve the frightening fever and knowing she would be physically incapable of dragging Julian from the bed and into a cold shower, Anne grabbed the sheet and carried it back into the bathroom. There she soaked it in cold water. Julian groaned when she covered him with the chilled, wet sheet and she wondered if she was doing the right thing. It had been so long since she'd had any first aid.

When the heat of his body had burned away the benefit of the wet sheet, she resoaked the material and applied it again. Julian didn't protest the damp cloth, but he continued to shift himself violently around on the bed and the muttered words became more and more difficult to comprehend.

"It hurts, ghost lady. It hurts. Can't tell anyone. Shouldn't even tell you."

"Where does it hurt, Julian?" Anne whispered, wondering if she ought to give him another tablet. If only she were absolutely positive they had been prescribed for this fever.

"My leg. It's bleeding. If I can't get it stopped...."

"Julian, the bleeding has stopped."

"No."

"Yes, darling. I've stopped it. You're going to be fine. Please believe me, darling. You're going to be fine."

Together with the damp sheets, she kept up the

running murmur of encouragement and reassurance for the next hour and then, when she was contemplating whether to risk another of the strange tablets, she sensed that Julian was finally growing quieter. In another hour she was certain the fever had broken. He was suddenly soaking wet and it wasn't from the effects of the damp sheet.

The sweat that coated his body was the aftermath of the fever. Carefully Anne stroked it from him and then she realized that she was going to have to change the saturated bedclothes. Now Julian would need warmth.

It was a chore remaking the bed because Julian had fallen into a deep sleep. He lay heavily in the middle of the damp bed and it took all of Anne's strength to roll him gently to first one side and then the other while she redid everything.

The room was quite cold now. The fire in the living room had probably gone out completely. She had been too busy to rebuild it. Anne went searching for a thermostat and finally realized there were some baseboard heaters in every room. Julian hadn't turned any of them on earlier, apparently. It took a long time before they became effective.

Anne spent the rest of the night keeping watch over her sleeping patient. At one point she thought he was growing warmer again and managed to wake him sufficiently to get another of the tablets down his throat. Then he began to complain of the cold.

At three in the morning chills were shaking his body and he clutched at her when she came near. The tawny eyes opened briefly, pleading with her.

"So cold," he growled. "Keep me warm, ghost lady. I need your warmth. So cold."

"Oh, Julian," she whispered, allowing herself to be dragged down beside him. There she gathered him to her, holding him beneath the covers until the chills stopped racking his body. Again he slept. When she was certain he was resting quietly she disengaged herself and went back to her chair.

At times during the early morning hours she dozed, but every shift in Julian's position, every change in his breathing pattern brought her back to full wakefulness. At dawn she finally abandoned any attempt at sleep for herself and, after checking her patient once more, went out into the kitchen to see about some tea or coffee.

The blanket of snow outside the window startled her. She had been so busy tending to Julian that she had forgotten the approaching storm. Her unwilling host had been right about one thing; she didn't have any chains in the car she had rented at the Denver airport. Until the roads were cleared she was trapped with her patient.

"As if I could leave him in his condition, anyway," she muttered resignedly, as she set a kettle on the stove. "Oh, Julian, what have they done to you?"

She didn't even know who "they" were. Just as she didn't know what had happened to the man who had captivated her so from the start of their short, stormy relationship. But she knew she would take great pleasure in seeking revenge for her lover of one night.

One night. Wryly she shook her head, wondering if Julian would even remember the passion that had reverberated between them. The fever had raged so swiftly that it was possible he wouldn't have any clear memory of the hour or two before it had seized him completely. The thought of how brilliantly his eyes had burned when he had opened the front door of the cabin made Anne wonder how ill he had been even then.

She had been so wrapped up in her anxiety and anticipation that she hadn't read the signs of illness in him until after he had made love to her. The realization made her wince. On the other hand what could she have done to halt the inevitable flow of the love-making once Julian had begun it? Nothing she could have said or done would have stopped him. Not then.

Carrying the pot of tea and a cup back into the bed-room, Anne sat down in the chair by the window and pulled the faded cotton drapes. Julian didn't stir as she poured herself a cup of tea and sipped thought-fully.

The thick layer of snow outside gave the mountains a deceptively serene appearance this morning. Stately fir and pine, heavily weighted with the white stuff made her think of postcard Christmases. She won-dered where Julian had planned to spend the holidays this year. Never in the short while she had known him had he mentioned any family or close friends. But then she knew so little about him. There had been no time to get to know each other before he and Mi-chael had left for that island. What she had learned of him and his background had made it painfully clear that there was no real hope for any kind of lasting relationship, even if the hostility between them could be appeased.

She wished there was a phone in the cabin. She could have called the pharmacy that had handled Ju-lian's prescription, and made certain she was using the tablets for the right symptoms. Uncertain and no longer desperate now that the fever had been drasti-cally reduced, she decided to hold off giving him any more medication until he was awake and coherent enough to tell her the pills were meant for this par-ticular purpose.

He slept throughout the morning and Anne de-cided the rest was more beneficial than waking him for some food. As soon as he was awake she would try to at least get some liquid down him.

Her own stomach began making demands around

nine o'clock, however, and Anne traipsed back into the kitchen to find something to eat. She was slicing some bread for toast when a faint noise made her swing around in surprise.

"Julian! You shouldn't be out of bed."

He stood in the doorway, staring at her. The fever had left him looking exhausted and a little unsteady, but the intensity of his gaze made her realize he was fully aware of his surroundings once again.

"I told myself I'd dreamed the whole thing," he whispered harshly.

"Julian, please go back to bed." Anne dropped the knife she had been using and went toward him trying hard to ignore the fact that he was standing stark naked in front of her. "You mustn't get chilled again."

"Are you sure you're not a ghost?"

"Quite sure." Perhaps he didn't remember everything that had happened during the night. It might be easier now if he didn't recall the lovemaking, Anne thought as she gently took his arm to lead him back to bed. Easier on her.

He ignored her hand, continuing to gaze at her in fascination. "You shouldn't be here. You're not supposed to be anywhere around here. You should be neatly tucked away back in Indiana doing research for that old professor who employs you."

"This way, Julian. I'll get you some breakfast if you like. Some poached eggs on toast."

This time he yielded to her firm tug, allowing himself to be led back to the tousled bed. She straightened it quickly and then urged him back between the covers. Somewhat to her surprise he obeyed, although he never took his eyes off her.

"Julian, are those tablets in the bathroom medicine chest for this kind of thing? I've already given you two of them but it says on the label you should have more."

"Two?" He frowned as he sank back into the pillows. His hand moved briefly across his eyes. "Only two?"

"Do you think you should have another one?" She plumped the pillows around him, bending over as she did so.

"No!" Then he relaxed a little. "No, not unless the fever comes back. It's never gone away this quickly, not even when I've taken the full dosage. Maybe... maybe I'm finally getting over...." His voice trailed off as she continued to fuss solicitously with the blankets. "Anne?"

"Yes, Julian?"

His hand came up to rest on her sweater right over the full curve of her breast. She froze, her eyes going anxiously to his intent face.

"Last night. I didn't dream any of it, did I? I carried you in here and made love to you."

Quite suddenly Anne knew she had been right earlier when she had wondered if everything would be much safer for her if Julian didn't remember the hour of passion.

"You were very ill last night," she soothed lightly, stepping out of reach of his hand. "In fact you were hallucinating at times, I think."

"Probably," he agreed dryly. "I usually do. But I didn't dream up that scene between you and me, did I?"

"I'm afraid so," she said gently, smoothing the hair back off his brow. She managed a nurse's smile. "You were ill when I arrived and it wasn't long after that before you were in bed."

"With you."

"Well, I was here," she admitted easily, "but not in a particularly romantic capacity. I spent a lot of time dampening sheets and soothing your fevered brow."

"Anne, I never would have guessed you were such

a little liar." He closed his eyes in weariness. "When I wake up next time you're going to tell me why."

He was asleep before she could think of a response. But as she stood looking down at the proud, tired lines of his face Anne told herself she would make an attempt to stick by her story. He had been delirious enough last night that he couldn't really be certain just what had been real and what had been a figment of his imagination.

She had been wrong using her brother's plight as an excuse to seek out Julian, Anne realized. It was true that she badly needed his help, but it had still been just an excuse to see the man who had haunted her memories for six months.

Julian Aries was like a wounded animal who would lash out at anyone who got too close. He needed time to heal his own wounds before a woman dared approach him to offer any kind of relationship. Even then she might find that he was incapable of real emotional commitment, let alone love.

Everything she had ever told herself about Julian was still true. He was a loner, a man who might pursue a woman in order to satisfy his desire for her, but who would never ask for or want feminine comfort or gentle concern.

If she'd ever needed proof of that, Anne thought, she had it now. Julian had retreated, sick and injured, to his lair after that last mission, preferring to lick his wounds alone.

She didn't try to fool herself. Anne knew very well that he wasn't going to be at all grateful for her nursing. When he came out of the aftermath of this fever he was going to be dangerous. He would be violently resentful of the fact that she had witnessed his weakness. Hurting as badly as he was he could easily turn on her and claw her, out of frustration and anger.

She'd had no right to track him to his lair, Anne

told herself grimly, and had no one but herself to blame for the mauling that was bound to ensue. Trapped here now, partly because of the snow and partly because there was no way she could leave while he was so helpless from the effects of the mysterious fever, she knew her only hope was to protect herself as much as possible.

There was no chance of coming out of the ordeal unscathed, but if she was very careful she might keep from getting completely lacerated.

3

THE FIRST WARNING SNARLS came around lunchtime when Anne carried a tray of hot chicken-noodle soup and a small sandwich into the bedroom. Julian's brooding gaze was on her the second she appeared in the doorway of his room, and she knew he had been waiting impatiently.

"I hate chicken-noodle soup."

"Then why do you have six cans of it on your kitchen shelves?" With a determinedly bright smile, Anne adjusted the tray in front of him. He sat back against the pillows, glaring at the soup bowl.

"I didn't feel like doing a lot of grocery shopping on the way up here. I just scooped up whatever was handy at the store in town."

"Winding up with six cans of a soup you don't like will teach you to be a more careful shopper in the future, won't it?" Anne observed cheerfully as she sat down in the chair beside the window to supervise his lunch.

He slanted her an assessing glance. There was clear menace in the catlike eyes but there were also traces of pain, and it was all Anne could do to keep from going over to the bed and cuddling him. Prudently she resisted the impulse, knowing she could easily get herself slashed in the process. Weak as he was, Julian was nevertheless dangerous, and she would be a fool to forget it.

"Shopping," he stated, "has never been one of my favorite hobbies."

"What are your favorite hobbies, Julian?" Anne demanded chattily. "I've often wondered if you have any. We know so little about each other."

"You discovered one of them last night." Morosely he picked up the soupspoon and tried a taste. "When uninvited females show up on my doorstep I take them to bed."

Anne astonished herself by not even flinching. "I'm afraid I must have missed something, then. You were flying high on that fever long before we ever reached the bedroom. Don't you remember how you kept complaining of the heat?"

"I remember how hot you were," he countered bluntly. "Compared to you, the fireplace was an iceberg."

"Your imagination certainly goes into overdrive when you're under the influence of that fever," Anne noted smoothly. "What is it, anyway? Malaria?"

"Something similar." He tried another spoonful of soup.

"Have you had many bouts of it? Those tablets in your medicine chest...."

"I picked it up on that damned island. It comes and goes."

"But how often has it recurred?" she persisted.

"Three or four times."

"What do the doctors say? How long will it continue to recur?"

"They don't know. With any luck the bouts will get less severe and eventually stop entirely. But I haven't been a real lucky man lately," he added derisively. "Unless you want to count last night, of course. I haven't thanked you for that, have I? I realize I might not have been at my best under the circumstances, but then, you didn't give me much notice. Give me a couple more days to recover and we'll try it again. That is, if you're still stranded here because of the snow."

"You can bait me all you want, Julian, but we both know I'm the only one who really remembers clearly what happened."

"Want to bet? How's this: You showed up on my doorstep last night to ask me for help with implementing some wild scheme of Mike's. You said Mike had been hit by a car and is still in the hospital and that you're planning on trapping the people you think tried to kill him. A bunch of ghost hunters, you said." He gave her a defiant look, daring her to tell him his memory wasn't clear on that subject.

"It was shortly after I told you all that, that you collapsed," she assured him gently.

"Like hell. But leaving that business aside for the moment, tell me more about this crazy plan. Are you serious about going through with it?"

"Yes."

"What does it involve?" he growled.

"Mike has already set everything up. Even if they're onto him, I don't think they'll have any way of being aware of his scheme. He's arranged for a very wealthy acquaintance of his, an eccentric old lady, to hire the ghost hunters. She wants them to clear out the family ghost from the mansion in California that she's just inherited. At least that's the story. She's going to swear she won't move in until the ghost has been, uh, freed from its mortal chains. I'm going to pose as her niece—her younger sister's daughter—who's volunteered to deal with the ghost hunters since 'auntie' won't come near the place until they've done their job. The house is full of valuable antiques and some really fine jewelry and paintings. It should be a sufficient lure for the theft ring."

"What happens after they've gone through their routine and left the mansion?"

"That's the part where I'm going to need a little help," Anne confessed. "I need someone who knows how to keep a house under surveillance and who can figure out how to catch the ghost hunters when they come back to steal the stuff they've decided they want."

He stared at her. "That part of the plan sounds a little vague," he noted dryly.

"It is. I think now that perhaps I'll hire a private detective," Anne explained assertively. "Private detectives ought to know about that sort of thing."

"You could wind up paying him for several months of surveillance. There's no telling when your psychic investigators will make their move. After all, if they've got keys or full information on the security system they can sneak back any time it's convenient for them. Presumably, long after anyone remembers that they were once in the house and thinks to connect them with the crime."

Anne drew a deep breath. "I'm supposed to let it drop casually during their first visit that 'auntie' is planning on installing a whole new electronic security system within a few weeks. Hopefully that will inspire the thieves to make their move quickly before all the locks are changed and the electronic detection stuff has been installed."

"I see."

Anne waited, expecting some sort of further comment. Even if he wasn't interested in getting involved in the scheme she thought he'd probably have some thoughts on the matter. But Julian said nothing, merely continuing to munch slowly on the sandwich. She realized he was tiring rapidly.

"Julian?"

"Ummm?" He appeared preoccupied.

"What do you think about Mike's plan? I'm not asking you to help me but I don't have anyone else with whom I can discuss it and I could use the advice. I admit I'm a little out of my field."

"Yeah."

Resentment prickled Anne. "Well, come to think of it, I doubt you've had a whole heck of a lot of experience trapping fake psychic investigators, either!"

"True. But I've seen a lot of carefully set traps go haywire, lady, and this particular trap doesn't even sound carefully worked out. With you in charge it's probably going to prove a total disaster."

Angrily Anne got to her feet. "If you've finished mauling that sandwich, I'll take the tray." She scooped it up before he could protest and swept out of the bedroom. She was trembling with outrage and a carefully imposed self-restraint. The last thing she wanted was to allow Julian to provoke a full-scale argument and that was what he was clearly bent on doing. He'd tried first to bait her with reminders of last night's passion, and then he was obviously intent on making her scheme appear foolish and unworkable. She had better learn that any opening she gave him for communication was an avenue he would twist for his own purposes.

It was as she washed out the soup bowl that she admitted to herself that she had really wanted his advice. She was out of her depth trying to implement Michael's plan and she knew it. Julian might be too occupied with healing his own wounds to help her carry out the plan but she'd been hoping for at least a few practical suggestions. She was nervous about what she was getting herself into, she realized. No, she was more than nervous. She was downright scared. The people she was hoping to trap had already shown themselves capable of attempted murder.

In the bedroom Julian collapsed more deeply into the pillows, closing his eyes in a combination of weariness and disgust. The fever always left him weak as a kitten, and the condition infuriated him. It was bad enough dealing with it on his own, but having

Anne witness it was the last straw. His fist clenched in helpless rage.

Why did she have to show up last night? Every time he had mentally planned his first encounter with her he had never intended it to happen that way. In all his fantasies on the subject he had never been on the brink of another bout of the fever. Nor had he still limped. And the scars had all been magically removed in his dreams.

He was right when he'd told Anne that he'd seen a lot of carefully set traps go haywire. The one he'd planned to set for her was a shining example. It was in ruins. The knowledge was maddening.

Everything was infuriating him this morning, his own physical weakness, the fact that Anne had been obliged to play nurse to him and the realization that she was determined to pursue her brother's idiotic scheme.

But the most infuriating thing of all was the way she calmly denied last night's passion.

He *knew* he hadn't dreamed up the lovemaking. No matter what she claimed this morning, he was sure of the way she had responded last night. Glowering savagely, Julian threw off the blankets and sat up on the edge of the bed. It took more energy than he had to spare, to make his way into the bathroom.

Leaning heavily on the sink he twisted so that he could see his shoulders in the medicine-chest mirror. Ignoring the slash of the scar he peered intently at the two tiny little scratches he had been only mildly aware of when they had been inflicted. They were small, only a few hours old and would undoubtedly disappear completely by the end of the day. But they were evidence.

Julian turned away from the mirror on a wave of rough satisfaction and staggered a bit as he made his way toward the bed. He hadn't been hallucinating when she had left those marks with her nails. He had been making love to his ghost, and furthermore, she had been responding.

But she was acting as if nothing at all had occurred between them. The question of why she chose to pretend he had dreamed it all up in a delirium kept festering in him.

Perhaps she was angry at him because of the way he had forced her into bed and then forced a response. He knew she had always been a little afraid of him, and the way he had treated her last night probably hadn't mitigated that fear in any way. Her surrender had been complete and she might have decided to deny it both to herself and to him. His fever had provided her with the perfect chance at regaining her pride.

Nursing him was bound to reinforce her sense of regained control. Between denying her response in his arms and being able to treat him like a helpless child this morning, she would be firmly reestablishing her sense of self-control in front of a man who had always threatened it.

Julian rubbed his aching head with his hand, grimly pleased with his own analysis of the situation. If she was still a little afraid of him and intent on denying her reaction to his lovemaking, perhaps his wounds and his weakness hadn't ruined everything. Perhaps she was not consumed with pity for him.

It was the one thing of which he had been so afraid: her pity. It was the last thing he wanted and the reason he had hidden himself in these mountains. He had planned to go looking for her when and if he healed. He had dreamed of returning to her as the strong, self-contained man he had been the last time he had seen her, not as a scarred weakling who was at the mercy of a malady that came and went with no warning.

The headache grew stronger, and Julian debated about taking another tablet. He decided against it. So far he'd only needed two of the pills, apparently. It would be a victory of sorts if he could get through the entire siege on that amount. Not much of a victory, but these days he had learned to take what he could get in the way of small triumphs.

A faint, savage smile briefly shaped his mouth. Actually he had two successes to celebrate this morning. In addition to getting by on only a couple of the tablets, he had his certain knowledge of the passion he had aroused in Anne. Her own denial of that arousal didn't detract from his sense of victory in the least. It meant she was still wary of him.

Six months ago he hadn't wanted her to be afraid of him but today he knew her signs of caution were signs of hope for him. A woman who was cautious around a man was subtly acknowledging his power. And as long as she thought he had some power over her, Anne wouldn't start pitying him.

In spite of the headache Julian was aware for the first time in months of the faint stirrings of a masculine arrogance he had once taken for granted.

Fifteen minutes later Anne had finished the few dishes left over from lunch and was frowning at the layer of dust on the well-worn furniture in the living room. For some obscure reason it annoyed her.

"Anne!"

Her frown intensified as she answered the summons. "What is it, Julian? Why are you out of bed?"

"Stop glaring at me." He stood braced in the bathroom doorway. "Don't we have any aspirin in the house?"

Anne deliberately stepped toward the bed and began tidying it. "I don't know. Do we?" she asked dryly. "I'm new here, remember?"

He swore softly and started back toward the bed,

clearly still shaky on his feet. "I guess I've used them all."

"Do you want another of those tablets in the medicine cabinet?" She kept her eyes averted from his unabashed nudity.

"No," he growled, crawling slowly back under the covers. The strain on his face told of his discomfort. "I just want some aspirin. I always get these damn headaches after the fever."

She eyed him dubiously, wondering if he shouldn't be taking his prescription tablets instead. "I was going to go out to my car and get my suitcase. I might have some aspirin with me. But, Julian, are you sure you shouldn't take some of your medicine?"

"Just get the aspirin," he ordered roughly, closing his eyes.

"You must be feeling better. You're back to issuing commands with your usual flair," she told him tartly.

"We'll get along fine if you just obey them." But the weariness in his voice spoiled the arrogant effect. The dark lashes stayed shut.

Anne's expression gentled as she realized how hard he was fighting to handle the pain and his own sense of weakness. "I'll be back in a few minutes," she promised.

Outside she found herself floundering through a foot of powdery snow. The crisp air was fresh and invigorating and the leaden skies were beginning to clear. The rental car was parked beside Julian's four-wheel-drive vehicle, and as she opened her trunk to remove her suitcase she wondered about using the more rugged truck to get down out of the mountains. Perhaps Julian would lend it to her if, in a couple of days, the roads hadn't been cleared.

There was no rush, she decided. For one thing she couldn't possibly leave Julian until she was sure he'd recovered enough to look after himself. And she still had a little time before she had to play the role of helpful niece in her brother's scheme. As she slammed the trunk shut and started back to the cabin with the suitcase, Anne realized just how glad she was to have the excuse of staying with her ill-tempered patient.

He was watching for her as she lugged the red leather bag into his bedroom. The tawny eyes were open now but there was a solid line of heavy eyebrows framing them. The leonine face was drawn tight with pain.

"Are you sure a couple of aspirin are going to do the trick?" Anne unlocked the red case and began going through it. The bottle was in a small zippered pouch.

"They'd better. That's all I'm going to take."

"Well, maybe if we combine them with a few other measures, you'll get some relief," she said, rising to her feet with the bottle of aspirin.

"What measures?" He looked somewhat suspicious as he swallowed the white tablets.

Anne smiled in what she hoped was a bright, nurselike fashion. "Turn over on your stomach and I'll give you a head and shoulder massage. That should loosen some of the tension and the pain."

Grumbling, Julian submitted to the pampering massage. "I used to do this for Michael occasionally," Anne explained as she sat beside him and moved practiced fingers over the knotted muscles of his neck and shoulders.

"Who taught you how to do this?" Julian gritted into the pillow.

"A friend of mine who's in the physical-education department at the college where I work."

"A male friend, I assume. Some ex-football hero?"

Anne hid a flicker of surprise at the note of challenge in his voice. "I don't believe Allen ever played football. He's the team's physical therapist, though, and he knows a lot about this sort of thing."

"I'll bet. Do you let him practice on you?"

"What is this," she asked lightly, "an inquisition?"

"Just trying to keep up my end of the conversation," Julian retorted. She could feel the beginning signs of relaxation in his neck, however. "You and this Allen date a lot?"

"A few times," she answered honestly. "Not a lot."

There was silence for a few minutes and then Julian asked, "Who else do you date in that ivory tower?"

"You can't be seriously interested in a list of people I go out with, Julian."

"The question has arisen in my mind at least once a day for the past six months," he rasped.

That stopped her for an instant. "It has?"

"Just answer the question," he said with a sigh.

"Well, occasionally I date a professor of history I've known for some time and then there's Allen. Once in a while I go out with Eric in the English department—"

"That's enough," Julian interrupted gruffly. "I should have known better than to ask for a list. For a quiet little research assistant you get around, don't you?"

She didn't care for the way he said that. "I realize my life-style lacks some of the excitement of yours, Julian, but in my own conventional fashion I manage to inject a little fun into my life."

"It sounds like it." There was another short pause. "Why haven't you ever married, Anne? Mike said you'd been engaged once."

"This really is turning into a game of twenty questions, isn't it?"

"Why aren't you married?" he persisted.

She gave a small shrug that he couldn't see and told him the truth. "It's just never quite worked out. My engagement ended when my fiancé told me he needed to be free to 'find himself.' He was in the philosophy department," she added by way of explanation. "Philosophers worry a lot about finding themselves, I discovered."

"Better for everyone if they stay lost," Julian muttered. "The world already has enough conflicting philosophies. Did your ex-fiancé ever succeed?"

"In finding himself? I don't know. He did, however, find a charming young female student in one of his classes who wanted to help him in the search."

"I see. You don't sound particularly upset over it."

"I'm not. That all happened about three years ago and it was all for the best."

"And since then?"

"Since then nothing's ever gotten beyond the casual stage," she admitted. *Except with you,* she added silently. *And you've made it clear you're not cut out for anything permanent.*

"I don't see how any man could remain casual toward you," Julian said thoughtfully. "You must be the one who keeps your dates at arm's length. Are you regretting the fact that you didn't manage to do that with me last night?"

Anne faltered as he made the deliberate reference to the passion she was trying to deny. "Poor Julian. That must have been a very interesting hallucination you had last night. How does your head feel?" she added crisply.

"Incredibly better," he admitted, sounding vaguely surprised.

"I'll convey your appreciation to Allen next time I see him," she couldn't resist saying as she got up from the bed.

"You do that," Julian countered, turning cautiously onto his back, golden eyes gleaming up at her with faint menace. "Right after you tell him how you spent the night with me."

"Allen would be the first to understand that someone had to play nurse to you last night," Anne managed sweetly.

The menace in his eyes grew a little stronger. "Go fix me some hot tea before I risk renewing the headache with a little physical exertion," he suggested meaningfully.

Anne fled to the kitchen, not knowing whether to be glad he seemed on the road to recovery or annoyed because of his quarrelsome manner. Memories of when he had clung to her, not in passion, but to still the chills that racked his body made the decision for her. She would be glad that he was recovering.

That altruistic attitude lasted only as long as the next challenge Julian issued, however. She had awakened him for his dinner, pleased to see that his color appeared much better than it had at noon. He sat up in bed, surveying the meal of curried stew and a thick chunk of bread. He looked as though he had the beginnings of an appetite.

"Did you make this?" he asked curiously.

"Well, it didn't come out of a can," she retorted, sitting down in the chair to eat with him. "I scrounged around in your freezer and found a package labeled lamb. You also had a sack of potatoes and some onions and carrots." She lifted one shoulder as if the result were inevitable.

"Not bad," he remarked grudgingy. "If you keep putting meals like this together I might let you stay for a while."

"Gee, thanks." She dipped her chunk of bread into the stew and took a bite.

He looked at her intently for a moment. "When do you have to be back at work?"

"I've got a month's leave of absence."

"Because of Mike?"

"Yes."

"But he *is* going to be okay, isn't he?" Julian asked slowly.

"The doctors say he'll recover. But it's going to be a long process. Fortunately he has Lucy."

"His fiancée, you said."

"That's right." Anne dipped the bread into the stew again, enjoying her own cooking and the knowledge that in spite of his grouchiness Julian was enjoying it, too.

"Then you don't have to rush back to his bedside."

"No."

He nodded. "You can stay here for a while, then," he finally said.

"Only a couple more days at the most. I have to be in California this coming weekend in order to set up Mike's plan," Anne explained.

"Don't be ridiculous. You're not going to get involved in that mess."

She glanced up from her stew, startled more by the absolute certainty in his voice than by the words themselves. "Julian, I've already told you that I'm going through with it."

"The answer is no."

She blinked. "I don't recall asking permission. Advice, maybe, but not permission."

He slid her a chilling glance. "If you think I'm allowing you to go through with that nutty plan all on your own, you're out of your head."

Anne arched one eyebrow, mildly surprised now by his interference. She had assumed he would be glad to see her leave. "I hate to break this to you, Julian, but you don't really have a whole lot to say about it."

"Someone had better say something about it," he

exploded softly. "Mike's apparently in no condition to do so. That leaves me."

"I told you, I came to ask you for help, not to get your permission to carry out the plan! It's obvious you're not in any condition to help me but I'm not going to cancel everything because of that. I'll find a way to make it all work."

Julian's bowl of stew was set down on the night-stand with a solid clunk. The next thing Anne knew, he was sitting on the edge of the bed, the blankets carelessly tossed to one side. One powerful hand reached out to take hold of her chin and the tawny eyes burned. Not with fever this time, but with male determination.

"I may not be at the peak of my physical ability and I may be a few months over forty, but if you think I can't handle you, lady, you're dead wrong. Last night should have taught you that much, at least."

She winced. "I think you're well enough to start remembering to put on a robe when you get out of bed in front of guests!"

"Why should I cover up what you've already seen?"

"Julian, stop acting as though you had some rights over me." She stood up abruptly and his hand fell away. "I intend to go through with Mike's scheme and I'm not going to let you stop me."

He got to his feet and, even though he had to flatten one hand against the wall to help him maintain his balance, he exuded more than enough intimidation to cause Anne to retreat uneasily.

"When are those ghost hunters supposed to show up at that mansion in California?" he asked too softly.

"At the beginning of next week."

"How long will they stay there?"

"Their usual routine lasts about three or four days," she answered carefully.

"Then you'll stay here where I can keep an eye on you until at least the end of next week. Until it's too late for you to do anything about that idiotic plan."

"I'm going through with it, Julian."

"No."

The cold denial infuriated her. "Where do you get off telling me I can't do as I damn well please? You have no authority over me, Julian Aries. Not one single right. I'm as free an agent as you are. You may recall that nothing I said or did could stop you from taking Michael to that island, and you made it very clear the night you brought him home that nothing could keep you from returning to finish your job. Well, I have a job to do now, too, and nothing you say or do is going to stop me."

He took a step toward her, releasing his hold on the wall. "There's no comparison between this crazy situation and the demands of my job six months ago!"

"Oh, yes there is," she countered, retreating to the doorway. "I'm as committed to carrying out this plan as you are to your precious supermacho career as a government agent. Michael was nearly killed by these people. I'm not going to let them get away with it!"

"Anne, you don't know what the hell you're doing," he raged.

"That's why I came here," she shot back. "To get a little help and advice. But since I'm not going to get either, I'll just have to muddle through on my own."

"I won't allow it!"

"You have nothing to say about it."

He stalked forward another step and Anne saw the effort it cost him. "Get back into bed, Julian. You need to rest," she said with sudden urgency, moving forward to take his arm. "Please, stop acting like this. You've been very ill and you have no business staging a major scene."

He didn't budge under her prodding. Instead his

hand moved around her nape and he held her as though she were an annoying kitten. "I will stage any kind of scene I please," he bit out savagely. "And, weak as I am, you're still not big enough or strong enough to stop me. Understand?"

The wounded lion was roaring now and Anne knew he was right about one fact. Even weak and in pain he could still overpower her if he chose.

"I understand, Julian."

"Good." He released her and staggered back to the bed, throwing himself down on it with a groan. Eyes closed he drew a deep breath. "We will discuss this further in the morning," he announced in a tone that was icy with the force of his effort to control it. "I'm going to get some sleep."

"Yes, Julian," Anne agreed meekly, knowing his head was probably throbbing again. She ached to be able to comfort him. Hurrying into the bathroom she picked up the aspirin bottle and a glass of water and carried both back into the bedroom.

Julian accepted the tablets gruffly after first making certain they weren't from the prescription bottle. Then he turned over on his stomach, burying his face in the pillow.

Without a word Anne sat down on the bed and began to massage his neck and shoulders again. He allowed her to minister to him as if he were tolerating a minor nuisance. But beneath her touch, she felt him begin to relax.

Poor lion, Anne thought with a small smile. He didn't know how to ask for a little tender loving care, not even when he needed it very badly. She wondered at the years of isolation and self-contained living that could breed such a fierce aloneness.

Julian Aries needed a wife and a home. But, then, she'd known that much six months ago. His refusal to accept his own needs made her wary of him.

"YOU'RE GOING TO GO through with it, aren't you?"

Two days later, ensconced on the living-room sofa with an old striped wool blanket over his legs, Julian acknowledged the inevitable. He was not, Anne decided, a gracious loser. It had been a hard-fought battle, she reflected. Julian had used almost every trick in the book except one.

He had tried to intimidate her, argued that he had an obligation to her brother to keep her out of trouble, informed her that she was not very bright, tried to order her obedience and had finally resorted to calm, rational discussion in an attempt to dissuade her. The one argument he had not tried was that she couldn't go through with the plan because he needed her to look after him.

Of course, Anne thought, that was the one tactic he never would use. Julian could not admit that he needed anyone, especially her. The certain knowledge filled her with a sense of hopelessness regarding their relationship. He wasn't the only one who needed to accept reality this morning, she thought as she finished washing the breakfast dishes. She needed a dose of it herself.

"I'm going through with it, Julian. I told you that two days ago."

"Even though I have absolutely forbidden the whole scheme?" he gritted.

"I thought you'd given up on the intimidation approach," she observed. "We were trying logic and reason the last time I tuned in."

"I gave up on both when you made it clear they weren't going to have much effect." Julian drank his coffee broodingly, his eyes never leaving her as she went about the kitchen chores. "I don't know why you're so dead set on this crazy plan. When your brother is out of the hospital he can renew his investigation and set up another scheme to trap those ghost hunters."

"I'm going through with it because I've got a good chance of making the whole thing work. They're on to Michael now. He won't be able to get close to them again. But they can't possibly know about me. And I don't think, from what I've learned about them, that they can resist the lure of old Miss Creswell's mansion. It's a perfect setup."

"There is no such thing as a perfect setup and if you'd had a little experience trying to carry out 'flawless' schemes, you'd know what I'm talking about!"

"I'm sure a little experience would be extremely useful, but I don't have time to get it."

"So you tried to take a shortcut by coming here to get my help and experience?"

She focused on the scene outside the kitchen window. The roads had been cleared that morning but the blanket of snow still made a postcard setting. "That was the general idea."

"The best advice I can give you is to stay out of it."

"That's the one piece of advice I'm not willing to take." She dried the plates and stacked them neatly on the cupboard shelf. "Just as you and Michael wouldn't take my advice not to go to that horrid little island six months ago."

There was a tense pause from across the room. Then Julian stated coldly, "It was my job to go. And it was Michael's job to come with me."

"I know that now," Anne said simply. "I've accepted the fact that both of you felt you had to go. I haven't blamed either of you for a long time."

"Is that the truth, Anne?"

"Yes."

"Are you sure that on some level you're not still hating me for what happened to your brother?"

"Michael made his own decision. I understand that now," she said quietly. "He also told me that you saved his life that night he got shot. After the sniper wounded him you risked your own neck to go out into the open and drag him back to safety."

"He would have done the same for me. Michael and I were in that mess together. We had a job to do."

"So do I."

"The hell you do! This isn't an assignment you have to carry out. You're doing this strictly to avenge Mike."

"Same thing," she shrugged.

"Anne, this is ridiculous. Mike can take care of himself. He can handle everything when he's back on his feet."

"That could be a long time. They hurt him very badly, Julian," she said starkly.

"All right!" Julian roared. "If you're going to be totally unreasonable about this, there's nothing I can do...."

"No."

"Except go with you," he concluded bluntly.

Anne lifted her head, startled. "Go with me? But, Julian, that's out of the question. I realized that the first night I arrived. You've got too much recovering to do. All I'm asking from you now is a little advice. Or perhaps you know someone who could help me. You must have some contacts."

"We'll leave tomorrow."

"Impossible! You're not coming with me." She tossed the dish towel down on the counter and faced him with her hands planted firmly on her hips.

"You've been very ill, Julian. You need rest. A lot of it."

"It's a stalemate, lady," he said wearily. "I can't stop you from going and you can't stop me from going with you. Both of us seem to have received an overdose of stubbornness somewhere along the line."

"Now you're the one who's being ridiculous, Julian. I am not going to allow you to come with me in your present condition."

He slanted her a glance that held mockery and menace. "What are you going to do? Tie me to the bed?"

"If necessary!" she shot back unwisely.

Julian was off the couch an instant later. The brown toweling robe he'd put on earlier at Anne's insistence flapped carelessly open as he swooped across the room. He reached her in three long strides, seizing her by the shoulders.

"The only way you can keep me in bed is by staying there with me," he gritted softly. "Anytime you want to repeat what happened between us that first night you arrived, just let me know."

"I've told you, nothing happened," Anne said very bravely, aware that she couldn't move under the grip of his hands.

"Don't give me that nonsense. We both know you wound up lying beneath me, all soft and sweet and on fire. I've been through enough hallucinations to know the difference between reality and dreams, Anne. Why do you keep denying what happened that night?"

Goaded, Anne lost her temper. "Because nothing did happen! I didn't come all this way just to go to bed with you. I wanted to talk to you, tell you about Michael. I wanted to apologize for the way I lashed out at you the night you brought him home. I wanted to see if we could put our relationship on a different

footing. I wanted a lot of things, but I didn't want to
go to bed with you."

"You're afraid of me, aren't you?" he asked.

The flicker of masculine satisfaction that she saw in
his eyes made her want to strike him. "Maybe I am in
some ways. It's only natural to be a bit cautious
around a man who won't admit he's human, that he
has needs like everyone else...."

"Oh, I'm willing enough to acknowledge my needs,
sweetheart," he whispered, pulling her against his
bare chest. The toweling robe had parted completely,
leaving only the snug-fitting jockey shorts as a shield
between Anne and Julian's overwhelming masculin-
ity.

"Julian, stop it. This isn't what I meant and you
know it."

But he ignored her, crushing her against the cloud
of curling hair that formed a shaggy triangle on his
chest. His lips came down on hers in a hard, punish-
ing kiss that effectively silenced any further argument. Anne felt the frustrated feminine fury welling
up inside, even as she acknowledged the effect of the
sensual punishment.

His mouth insisted on her cooperation, his tongue
probing arrogantly into the dark, warm recesses behind her teeth. It wasn't until she gave up trying to
fight him and instead leaned obediently against him
that Julian lifted his head. The tawny eyes softened as
he stared down into her defiant face.

"Now why don't you stop pretending that nothing
happened between us the other night?"

"You indulge your fantasies, I'll indulge my own,"
she said bravely.

"Little coward." He was more amused than anything else by her bravado. Slowly, this time with
compelling invitation, he lowered his mouth once

more to hers. His hand moved lightly to her hips, shaping her with possessive, sensual care until she moaned softly. Then he deliberately cupped her buttocks and lifted her up into his hard thighs.

"Julian." Anne sighed and nestled closer out of sheer instinct. Fighting him was so very difficult. Her fingers clung to the warmth of his sleek back beneath the robe and she knew a shiver of need as he made her fully aware of his own mounting desire.

"I could take you so easily, make you want me...."

"Julian, please don't...."

"If you're afraid of me even though I'm in this condition, how are you going to deal with something really frightening such as that theft ring you're intent on trapping?" He nuzzled her nape, cradling her head against his shoulder.

"I'll manage," she gasped, intensely aware of the hardness of his body. The insistent pressure of his aroused male form was both a lure and a challenge that was as old as time. But she knew she had to resist. And he must have sensed it.

With resignation, Julian dropped his hands and stalked back to the couch. The limp was more pronounced now and she knew he was struggling to control it. "When you pack for me this afternoon, don't forget my razor or the can of shaving cream." He leaned his head back against the pillow and promptly went to sleep.

Anne stood staring at him for a long moment wondering how she was going to deal with all the ghosts, real and imagined, that seemed to have invaded her life. Chief among them was the ghost of a dream she had believed in for the past six months; a dream of building a lasting relationship with Julian Aries. She had been a fool to think this man would ever admit that he needed her on any level except a

sexual one. The lion had been surviving on his own
for too long. He was not going to risk the weakness of
loving and needing.

Slowly Anne went into the bedroom to pack Julian's clothes for the trip west. She knew him well
enough to know that he would be with her when she
left tomorrow morning, regardless of what it cost him
in terms of pain or exhaustion.

AT DAWN THE NEXT MORNING Anne stirred on the sofa she
had been using as a bed since she had no longer felt it
necessary to keep a watch over her patient. A sense of
presence in the room made her open her eyes, and
she stared in astonishment at Julian who was fully
dressed and prowling around the kitchen, making
coffee.

"Good grief," she complained, yawning hugely as
she pushed back the blankets. "You're up early."

He threw her a quick glance before going back to
the coffee preparations. "From what you've told me
we have a long trip ahead of us and a lot to do after
we arrive at the other end."

"Well, yes, but I didn't say we had to rise at the
crack of dawn."

"When I'm not coming out of a bout of that damn
fever, I usually get up at dawn," he said, shrugging.
"Sometimes earlier."

"Part of the secret-agent ethic?" she grumbled,
stumbling to her feet. Her long flannel nightgown
floated around her ankles. "Early to bed, early to rise,
helps a guy catch villainous spies?"

"That's not too bad, considering just how early it is.
Are you always that fast at this hour?"

"No. I was briefly inspired." Anne patted another
yawn, suddenly aware of how disheveled she probably looked. Her hair was a tousled, russet mop and
the flannel gown had been chosen for warmth, not

seductiveness. Not that she wanted to seduce Julian, she reminded herself grimly. "Actually, you're looking fairly perky yourself, this morning. You must feel better."

He considered that. "I do, as a matter of fact. Better than I have in a long time." The information seemed to surprise him. He frowned and flipped on the coffeepot switch.

He did look good this morning, Anne thought as she hurried down the hall toward the bathroom. He was wearing a gray sweater, a pair of jeans and boots. His dark hair was clean from the shower and had been ruthlessly combed into place. Julian moved this morning with something approaching his former lithe grace, even though the limp was still hampering him. There was a sense of regained strength in the leanness of his body.

Anne was seriously asking herself whether or not she could take any credit for his sudden progress when she realized the probable truth. Julian was looking better and feeling better this morning not because of her careful nursing but because for the first time in months he was about to go back to work. He had a task ahead of him. A self-imposed task, to be sure, but a real one.

The realization was depressing. She should be glad that he might finally be showing some signs of enthusiasm, she told herself. After all, apparently he had been holed up here for the past several months, licking his wounds. His mental outlook must have been very dark indeed during that period. Perhaps a challenge was exactly what was needed right now to help complete his recovery.

But deep inside, Anne knew the notion wasn't nearly as heartwarming as it should have been. The reality of the matter was that she had been nourishing a secret hope that she would be the cause of his recovery. She had wanted him to need her. When was she going to stop building up her hopes, Anne wondered sadly.

Julian was accompanying her to the West Coast for a variety of reasons, but none of those reasons included love. He probably felt an obligation to protect Michael's sister, since he hadn't been able to talk her out of the scheme. And he might be finding some inner enthusiasm for the unexpected challenge. But he wasn't going with her because he had finally realized he was hopelessly in love with her.

Anne grimaced at her own crazy emotionalism and drowned her discontent under the pulse of the shower spray.

"There are a few ground rules we'd better get straight before we get on that jet," Julian announced a couple of hours later, as he locked up the cabin and held out his hand for the keys to the red Buick Anne had rented at the Denver airport.

"Such as?" Anne ignored his outstretched hand and opened the door on the driver's side.

"Such as the one about me being in charge of this crazy project." Deftly he snapped the keys from her fingers. "Get in on the passenger side, Anne. I'll do the driving."

"The car is rented in my name. I'm the only one authorized to drive it," she protested, annoyed with the way he was starting to take over completely.

"Those roads are going to be slippery. Icy in places. Something tells me you haven't had a whole lot of experience driving a mountain road after a snowstorm."

"The roads have been cleared!"

"They'll still be treacherous. Get in on the other side, Anne."

Grumbling about his tyrannical attitude, Anne did as she was told, making a production out of tightening her seat belt while he started the car. "You're certainly in fighting trim this morning. But then, you always were inclined to give orders."

"Yeah." He shifted into reverse and expertly backed the car out of the drive, which had been only roughly cleared by a helpful road crew. "I've always been inclined to give orders. Not take them. I'm made that way, honey. It's one of the reasons I usually work alone or with only a partner."

"Well, think of me as a partner," she retorted.

"Even when I have one, I'm the one in command. I mean it, Anne. You're way out of your depth in this business with the fake psychics and you know it. If this idiotic plan is going to have any chance at all it will be because you understand and follow my orders. Got it?"

"If I'd known you were inclined to be such a tyrant I would have thought twice about asking for your help."

"You know anybody else you could have asked?" he countered smoothly. "Your good buddy Allen, the physical therapist, perhaps? Or the guy from the English department? Something tells me you didn't go pounding on their doors before you tried mine, did you, Anne?"

"I'm sure if I had, they would have proved far more cooperative," she muttered.

"You don't need cooperation. You need effectiveness." His mouth hardened as he negotiated an icy curve. "I'm generally considered effective."

Anne felt a chill down her spine at the way he said it. "You talk as if you're an instrument or a tool that someone uses."

"That's pretty much what I was to the people I worked for, I guess," he said with an offhandedness that alarmed Anne.

"And that's the way you thought of yourself, too,

wasn't it?" Before he could respond, she hurried on, frowning at his profile. "What's with the past tense? You're not officially employed any longer?"

"No."

"I didn't realize you'd quit your job," Anne said uncertainly.

"It was a mutual decision," he said coolly. "Both I and my employers realized that my effectiveness had been somewhat blunted at least as far as fieldwork goes. Forty-year-old agents who aren't as fast on their feet as they once were and who are prone to unpredictable bouts of incapacitating fever don't make good tools."

She heard the self-disgust in his voice and her own words were charged with sudden fierceness. "Well, it sounds to me like your career has taken a definite step forward. What an awful thing to think of yourself as a tool to be used by others."

"Happens all the time," he said, the words slicing through her like a knife. "Isn't that why you showed up on my doorstep a few days ago? Because you needed a convenient instrument to help you with your grand scheme?"

Anne went white under the shock of the sardonic accusation. The lion's claws were definitely not sheathed. In spite of the uneasy pact between herself and Julian, she was going to get mauled occasionally. The beast was still very dangerous. She wondered bleakly if he even realized just how much damage he could do to her. She was only beginning to realize how vulnerable she was.

"I didn't want to *use* you, Julian," she whispered.

"No?" He threw her a laconic smile. "Let's think of the arrangement as a bargain then, hmmm? I'll do my best to help you implement Mike's plan and in return...."

She slanted him a wary glance. "In return?" she finally prompted.

"How about in return I get a few more of those rather interesting hallucinations like the one I had the night you arrived at my door?" he suggested.

A dark red stain replaced the paleness in Anne's cheeks. She studied the mountain landscape intently while her anger simmered. "I don't need to pay you off with fantasies. You've already proved you can dream up your own."

"Anne—"

She interrupted him with quiet savagery. "If and when I go to bed with you, Julian, and it's a mighty big 'if,' I promise you it won't be because I'm paying you off for your 'effectiveness.' And I think you know it."

"Do I?" he drawled gently.

"One thing's for certain," she got out, almost choking on her fury, "until you do know it, you had better believe you don't stand a chance of sharing my bed! I won't make love to a man who thinks I'm repaying him for services rendered."

"Then what shall I think the next time you give yourself to me?" he inquired blandly.

"I think," Anne told him imperiously, "that you had better concentrate on your driving. You were quite right about the road. It's very treacherous." *Almost as treacherous as you, my wounded love.*

He appeared satisfied at the small sign of retreat. Anne's irritation increased by several degrees. The only positive note in the whole situation as far as she could see was that Julian definitely looked healthier and stronger this morning. Apparently the aftereffects of the fever didn't last long.

"Tell me about the ghost," he said at one point after they had left the mountains and were on their way into Denver. "I thought all the real ghosts in the country were on the East Coast. Since when does California have ghosts?"

"California's history is every bit as interesting as

that of the East Coast. The Spanish colonized it in the seventeen hundreds, and over the years a lot of legends have developed. We needed a house that had a genuine legend attached to it because the fake psychics will check that part out. Our ghost is Spanish, by the way. A charming young señorita who apparently had a mind of her own. It was a problem for women in her day. Got her into a lot of trouble, according to the tale."

"Figures the ghost would be female."

"I researched the story before I came to see you. Even though it's all nothing more than a legend, I wanted to get the details straight. I'm sure Thomas Craven and his friends will do the same thing."

"Craven?"

"He's the one in charge of these so-called psychic investigators. According to my brother's notes he works with a woman called Sara and a man called Dan Hargraves. Sara's the 'sensitive' of the group."

"She's the one who's actually supposed to be able to detect the presence of the ghost?"

"Right. She makes the contact and finds out what it will take to free the phantom from its mortal ties so that it can go wherever released ghosts are supposed to go. Beyond the veil or something. Thomas Craven and the man called Hargraves are the ones who then go through the rituals. Apparently the three of them can put on a pretty good show. Should go down well in California," Anne concluded sardonically.

"Have they worked out there before this?"

"According to Michael's notes, no, they haven't. As you said, most of the more interesting ghosts tend to be on the East Coast. Most of Craven's psychic investigations have taken place back there."

"How did your brother lure Craven out west?"

"Michael got an old acquaintance of his to arrange it. Someone he met when he was researching psychic phenomena agreed to help him set the trap. Miss Creswell's a strange old lady who had a sister who was a film star back in the thirties. The sister owned the mansion near Santa Barbara where we're going. She died a couple of years ago and left the place to Miss Creswell. Miss Creswell has agreed to let it be known that she plans on moving into the place in a few months and wants the mansion thoroughly de-ghosted. She's the one who actually hired Craven and his crew. And she's informed them that her niece will be their hostess. She herself won't come near the place until it's properly cleansed of ghosts. At least that's the story my brother got her to tell. Actually, she's very much into psychic phenomena herself. Can't stand phonies."

"And that's why she agreed to help your brother set the trap." Julian shook his head. "What a half-baked scheme. Who was originally supposed to play the role of niece?"

"Lucy Melton. My brother's fiancée."

"You jumped in and volunteered to take over so she could stay with Mike while he's recovering, I suppose."

"That's right. Why are you so negative about this?" Anne demanded in annoyance.

"Hasn't it occurred to you that if Craven and crowd have already made an attempt on your brother they're probably on to his plan to set them up?"

"They didn't cancel. Miss Creswell heard from them just before I left for Colorado. Craven gave her the date of his arrival," Anne informed him haughtily. She was getting distinctly tired of his obvious opinion of the project. "Besides, there's no way they could connect my brother with Elizabeth Creswell. Michael was very careful to keep himself out of the picture."

"So why did someone run him down in a car?" Julian asked politely.

"Probably because they decided Michael was getting too close to the truth. He told Craven he was doing a story on psychic investigators, and Craven allowed him to accompany his crew on a few investigations. Those all took place back East. Craven must have gotten suspicious about Michael's real interest, namely the thefts that seemed to follow in the wake of an 'investigation.' But there's no reason to think Craven knows the California arrangement has been set up by my brother."

"Maybe. Maybe not. Mike's good, I'll grant that. It's possible he kept his connection with Creswell secret and that Craven will be lured into the trap. But the whole thing sounds highly reckless and the only reason I'm having anything to do with it is because you've made it clear you're going through with it on your own if I don't. I meant what I said, Anne. You're going to follow my orders and you're going to do exactly as I say without demanding a lot of explanations and reasons. Clear?"

"I appreciate your help in this matter and I will endeavor to cooperate with you in view of your vastly superior knowledge," Anne murmured sarcastically.

He shot her a mildly amused glance. "You're cute when you're trying to be arrogant."

"You're not."

"Cute?" He thought about that. "No, I don't suppose I am. I don't think anyone's ever called me 'cute' in my whole life."

"Then it's fortunate you never had to make your living as a male stripper, isn't it?" Anne retorted too sweetly. "Look, Julian, I'm willing to be reasonable about this and I do respect your, uh, unique abilities in certain areas. I'm prepared, for example, to admit you may know a lot more about handling unsavory characters such as Craven and his bunch...."

"Thanks. Always nice to have one's talents admired."

"Nevertheless," she continued, undaunted, "I want you to keep in mind that this is my plan and I have as much, or more, to say about how it's implemented as you do!"

"No."

"What do you mean, no?" she challenged.

"It's a simple enough word. Your problem is that you probably haven't heard it used too often. Do you always get your own way, Anne? Mike told me you've always been on the bossy side."

"Younger brothers always say that about their older sisters."

"Yeah, but in your case it was true, wasn't it? Had to be, from what Mike said. You had a lot of responsibility to handle after your folks split up. Your father disappeared from the picture entirely and your mother's new country-club husband didn't much care for a couple of teenagers around the house. Mike told me you moved out when you were barely eighteen and he went to live with you. He was only fifteen at the time, wasn't he?"

"You and my brother appear to have had some lengthy little chats." Anne kept her gaze on the roadside scene.

"You got Mike through some rough years," Julian went on musingly. "Made sure he went to college. Kept him out of trouble. You had a lot invested in him emotionally. No wonder you hated my guts when I asked him to go with me on that last mission."

"Could we get back to the original discussion?" Anne moved restlessly in her seat. "There's not much point talking about what's over and done. I've told you that I understand now that nothing could have kept Michael from going with you. He thrives on the excitement of going after the story. It's in his blood."

"Intellectually I think you do understand that. But how about emotionally? Are you sure you're not still blaming me for what happened to him on that island?"

"No, Julian," Anne said patiently, "I'm not still blaming you." She was secretly surprised that he was worrying about it. He knew he wasn't responsible for what had happened to Michael six months ago. So why should he care about her reaction?

"All right. Back to the previous topic," Julian said evenly. "There really isn't much more to say about it. I'll be the one in charge."

"Don't I even get to vote on the matter?" she taunted.

He lifted one dark brow. "No."

"Concise and to the point. Okay, Julian, it would appear I don't have a lot of choice. You're in charge."

To her astonishment he threw her a quick grin, the first wholehearted expression of amusement she had witnessed in him since she had arrived at his cabin. "Being in charge of you should prove interesting." The brief laughter in his eyes disappeared almost immediately as he gave his attention to his driving again.

Anne was not at all surprised by his skill on the uncertain road surface. There was a fundamental competency and efficiency in the man that was an integral part of him. They were qualities that had allowed him to survive on his own in life and she wondered if, after forty years of depending on them rather than on other people, Julian could ever change. He would probably always be too proud to ask for love. She accepted that now. What worried her was the possibility that he would never even be able to accept his need of a woman on any other level than a sexual one.

There was little conversation for the rest of the trip.

Julian was engrossed in his own thoughts and Anne maintained a respectful silence. She knew he was sorting through the information she had given him, looking for problem areas and trying to modify the plans where possible.

By the time they had turned in the rental car and bought the tickets for Los Angeles, Anne knew Julian was beginning to tire. She saw the lines of strain around his eyes and fretted. But there was nothing she could say or do. He wouldn't appreciate having the weakness pointed out and she knew it.

As he sank down into the seat beside her and buckled the seat belt he finally allowed himself to relax. Anne said nothing, but she watched him uneasily out of the corner of her eye as he leaned back against the headrest and closed his eyes. Perhaps she should get him some coffee from the cabin steward. Then again he might need the sleep. She was chewing anxiously on her lower lip, wondering how to comfort him without annoying him when Julian spoke. He didn't bother to open his eyes.

"One other thing, Anne...."

"Yes?"

"How did you plan to explain me?"

"To Craven?"

"Right. He's expecting Miss Creswell's niece but he won't be expecting me. When your brother's fiancée, Lucy, was going to play the part, was she going to be alone in the house?"

"Yes, except for the housekeeper who comes in on a daily basis. Michael didn't think there would be any danger to Lucy. Craven's only interested in getting the layout of the place and earmarking the valuable stuff. Mike planned to stay in a motel in Santa Barbara. Lucy could have called him if she got nervous."

"So Craven's going to arrive and find the niece he

expected but also a man he didn't expect to see. We need a story to cover my presence in the house."

Anne's mouth tilted upward as a shaft of mischief went through her. "Well, actually, I did have one rather clever idea."

"Ummm?"

"How about if we dress you up in a suit and tell Craven you're the butler?"

Julian's eyes opened at that. He stared at her. "The butler! Are you serious?"

"You don't like it?"

"Do you really think I'd pass as a butler?" he growled.

"Aren't you clever agent types trained to be adaptable?"

"Ex-agent," he corrected curtly. "And, no, I wasn't trained to be that adaptable."

"Pity. It would have been rather amusing to see you running around in a suit fetching sherry for me."

"You'll have to get your kicks some other way, I'm afraid," he told her flatly.

"Well, we could pretend you're Miss Creswell's insane nephew who's been hidden away for years in the basement of the mansion."

"Your imagination is taking my breath away." He shut his eyes again. "Any other bright ideas?"

Anne's urge to tease him faded as she saw the weariness in him. He had seemed so much better this morning but it was obvious he was tired now after the long drive out of the mountains. He needed some rest. "There was one other, uh, possibility," she began tentatively. "Not as brilliant and original in concept as my first two ideas, but—"

"Let's hear it."

"It occurred to me that you could pose as my fiancé or lover or male friend, or whatever you want to call it," she said, stumbling over the words. "It would give you an excuse for being with me. Craven could think that the two of us were simply taking advantage of auntie's little task to enjoy a few days together at the mansion. You know, that we were making a short vacation out of it."

The dark lashes stirred on his cheek but he didn't open his eyes. "Your fiancé," Julian mused. "Yeah. I like it. We'll go with that."

He was asleep before Anne could start on her long list of why it wasn't such a good idea.

5

"THE MANSION WAS BUILT on the ruins of an old adobe hacienda," Anne explained late that night as she and Julian finished the long drive from the Los Angeles airport to the Creswell estate just outside Santa Barbara. "The original owners had received a land grant from Spain that extended from the coast to a point several miles inland. The hacienda was destroyed in an earthquake sometime during the eighteen hundreds, and the present mansion was built in the early nineteen hundreds. A lot of movie-star wealth and a certain amount of Hollywood tackiness went into the place according to Lucy, who talked to Miss Creswell. Lucy said she wants a full report on each of the bedrooms and the master bath, by the way. Apparently the designer was given free rein and a large budget."

"I can't wait." Julian negotiated the coastal highway, following the directions Anne read off to him. He looked much better again, she noted with relief. The nap on the plane had helped. All in all her patient was coming along quite nicely.

The realization that she was secretly taking credit for his improvement made Anne smile to herself in the darkness of the car. Julian had not offered one word of thanks for her nursing skills and attention but, knowing how much he had resented her arrival, she wasn't expecting any great show of appreciation.

"So our ghost is a holdover from the days when the old hacienda stood on this land?" Julian asked as they turned off the main road to wind up toward a high bluff overlooking the sea.

"Yes, according to my research poor little Carlota was the victim of an arranged marriage. Her parents sent her off to the wilds of California to marry a very wealthy landholder who was several years older than she was and who had already been married and widowed. She not only acquired a husband, she also acquired his three children and the responsibility of running the huge hacienda. She was only a teenager at the time."

"I can sense trouble brewing already," Julian groaned. "Young wife resents being tied down to an older husband and his three kids. Longs for the bright lights of wherever it was she came from."

"Mexico. Hers was a wealthy, landed family down there. Lots of old Spanish pride. And if we are to believe the legend, she longed for more than lights. She also apparently missed some of the admirers she left behind. Carlota was, from all accounts, a very lovely young woman and accustomed to a great deal of masculine attention."

"Let me guess. She found someone here in California who made up for the lack, right?"

"How did you know?"

"I could see it coming a mile away," Julian said wisely.

"I didn't know you were such an authority on the female psyche," Anne observed with interest.

"I'm not. But the only reason there's a ghost story left to tell is that Carlota somehow met with disaster, right?"

"Right."

"Given the other ingredients of the story so far, I think it's fair to assume that the most likely sort of disaster for sweet little Carlota to have precipitated was of the male-female variety. In other words, she got bored running the hacienda and started fooling around."

"Hardly fooling around," Anne said with a sniff, feeling obliged for some reason to defend the other woman. "She got involved in a grand, utterly hopeless love affair with the dashing young son of the owner of the neighboring ranch."

"Bet I know what happens next. Carlota and lover are discovered in a more or less compromising position by Carlota's husband and...?"

"And her husband killed her. Strangled her to death with his bare hands," Anne concluded sadly.

"I expect her husband was a little upset at the time," Julian pointed out, sounding totally unsympathetic toward the unknown Carlota. "What happened to her lover?"

"He escaped. His family shipped him back to Spain as fast as possible, apparently. Typical that only the woman in the triangle got punished."

"She must have known the risk she was taking. Husbands aren't noted for their tolerance in these matters. Not even today."

"You're an expert on that subject, too?" Anne demanded.

"Let's just say I have a vivid imagination, okay? I have no trouble picturing how I'd react in a similar situation."

He sounded so utterly sure of his own reaction that Anne was rather startled. "You're forty years old and have never been married," she complained. "How do you know what you'd feel if you were a husband in that situation?"

Julian shrugged. "I just know how I'd react."

"You'd have strangled poor Carlota?" Anne was suddenly feeling inexplicably incensed.

"Well, I don't know that I would have gone that far," Julian admitted easily. "But I certainly would have beaten you to within an inch of your life."

"Beaten *me!*" Anne stared at him, aghast. "We're not talking about me. We're talking about some poor woman who lived over a century ago. We weren't discussing *me!*"

"Oh. Perhaps it's just my new role of fiancé that has given me an insight into the matter. I might have been overempathizing," he remarked dryly.

"It sounds like it," Anne snapped back tartly. "Now, to finish the story. The reason Carlota occasionally appears in the mansion, according to legend, is that she's looking for something."

"What?"

"No one knows. I expect Mr. Craven and his bunch will be only too happy to tell us, however."

"And, since the legend doesn't tell us exactly what she searches for, Craven can simply make up that part, right?"

"Right. It will be interesting to see what creative touches he'll add to the story. Look, there's the place, now." Anne leaned forward to peer at the large structure looming up out of the night.

"You were right about the Hollywood touch. Looks like something off the back lot of a movie studio," Julian decided as he parked the rented car in the wide, circular drive.

The lines of the mansion were vaguely classical but the designer had obviously been unable to resist throwing in some originality. The overall effect was of a storybook mansion, composed of elements drawn from several different architectural periods.

"I'll bet the original adobe structure was more attractive. I wonder how Carlota likes having this thing sitting on the ruins of her home." Anne opened her door as Julian switched off the ignition. "It doesn't look as though the housekeeper is here. I don't see any lights." She rummaged through her purse, searching for the key she had collected from Lucy.

Julian stood patiently with the luggage as Anne

sounded the huge brass door knocker. When there was no answer, she used the key to let them into the wide hall. There she fumbled briefly before finding the light switch. She and Julian stood in silence, staring at the surroundings.

"I think," Julian finally commented as he surveyed the intricate oak parquet floor, the huge, multitiered crystal chandelier and the carved staircase at the end of the hall, "that I like my cabin better."

"Personally I'm reserving judgment until I see the bedrooms." Anne headed determinedly for the staircase. "Here, I'll take my own suitcase," she added quickly as Julian made to follow her.

He must not have appreciated the expression of concern in her eyes because he ignored her outthrust hand. "I'll manage," he growled. "I might not be up to carrying you up these stairs, but I can still handle a couple of suitcases!"

Anne held her tongue, unwilling to say more and risk another dose of his irritation. He must be quite tired by now, she told herself. Better not to provoke him. Actually, all things considered, it was always better not to provoke Julian. A dangerous pastime.

The housekeeper might not have been in evidence but it was obvious she had recently been on the scene. The half dozen bedrooms were all immaculate and fully prepared. It was clear immediately where the designer had drawn his inspiration.

"Good heavens! Each bedroom looks like a scene from a film," Anne gasped as she opened doors.

"Yeah. A love scene," Julian agreed laconically as he stopped to peer into what looked as if it could have been a stage set of Cleopatra's bedroom. The one across the hall was straight out of a thirties musical. Black-and-white stairs led up to a black-and-white canopied bed. "Which one do you want?"

"This one, I think," Anne declared with abrupt decision as she opened the last door on the right. "Definitely this one."

Julian came to stand behind her. "Well, I'll be damned. I never would have pictured you as the harem type."

"Ah, but this isn't a harem scene. This is the sheikh's tent from one of those Rudolph Valentino films," Anne announced as she walked cautiously into the flamboyant room. "Isn't it incredible?"

Hollywood's vision of exotic, Middle Eastern splendor reigned supreme in the gaudy room. The ceilings and walls were draped with an elaborately printed fabric. The bed was a huge round affair so covered with tasseled pillows that it was difficult to tell where it began and where it ended. Gossamer veils cascaded down over the bed from a wrought-iron hook in the ceiling. Underfoot an intricately designed rug completed the opulent effect.

"Are you sure this is the room you want?" Julian appeared doubtful. He began prowling around, opening the mirrored closet doors.

"Are you kidding? I'll probably never have another chance to sleep in something like this as long as I live. A once-in-a-lifetime opportunity," Anne enthused. She picked up her red leather bag and set it on a nightstand. "Which room are you going to use?" she asked as she began pulling out her toothbrush and a robe.

A moment later when he still hadn't answered she glanced up to see him watching her curiously.

"Well?" Anne prompted expectantly.

"We decided to pass me off as your fiancé, remember?"

"So?"

"So, I'll sleep in here. If you're really sure this is the room you want," Julian added in resignation. He eyed the draped bed morosely.

Anne took a deep breath, telling herself to take it carefully. There was something rather substantial about him as he stood in the middle of the fantasy room. In his gray sweater and dark jeans, he appeared as a solid, rather forbidding note against all the ornamental splendor of the bedroom.

"Julian, you're playing the *role* of my fiancé. You are not actually going to marry me, if you'll recall," she said dryly. "Our engagement is as much a piece of fiction as this room itself is."

He moved forward slowly, tawny eyes darkening. "What's wrong with a little fantasy, lady? Didn't you enjoy the dream we shared that night you arrived at the cabin?"

"Julian...." Anne stepped hastily back as he lifted a hand to stroke the side of her cheek. "Go find a room of your own. You're not staying here."

His expression darkened. "Craven will be suspicious if we're not sleeping together."

"No, Craven will not be suspicious. Why should he be? A lot of couples maintain a certain image of propriety during an engagement," she snapped.

"You and I," he stated with grave certainty, "would definitely be sleeping together. And I wouldn't care who knew it. I'd want everyone to know."

"Craven doesn't have to know you feel so strongly on the subject," Anne reminded him rather tartly. Matters were getting dangerous. Julian seemed to have convinced himself that playing the part of her fiancé automatically gave him a few rights. No wonder he had jumped at the idea when she had mentioned it on the plane. "If you don't climb down out of your macho tree, we will revert to plan B," she waned.

"What's plan B?"

"That's the one where you get to play the role of the insane nephew who's been kept in the basement for forty years. I always did have a preference for plan B!"

Julian's expression hardened and the hand on her cheek slid down to her shoulder where it faintly tightened. "Why do you fight me? You know you want me."

"Do I?" she challenged, stepping out from under his hand to return to her unpacking. A faint shiver of anticipation or fear moved through her as he once more closed the distance between them. She refused to glance up at him. The menace Julian was radiating was suddenly filling the room.

"Even if you won't admit that you want me, there's something else you can't deny," he said grimly.

"What's that?" Carefully she unfolded a white, long-sleeved shirt.

"Just the little matter of the fee for my services—"

He never got a chance to finish what he was going to say. Anne didn't even pause to consider her own response. She swung around in one swift movement, her right palm colliding against the side of his face in a violent slap that caught him totally by surprise.

"Don't you ever, *ever* imply that I would buy your help that way! You might be willing to sell your expertise that cheaply, but I'm not willing to pay that price. I would only sleep with you for one reason, Julian Aries, and it's got nothing to do with paying you off. If you bring up that possibility one more time I swear I will...I'll push you off that cliff out there!" The muted pulse of the surf far below the bedroom window backed up her enraged promise.

Julian narrowed his eyes. The mark of her hand was turning a dull red on his cheek and jaw but he made no effort to touch the injured area. Anne realized she was breathing much too quickly and that the adrenaline was pounding through her bloodstream. She was furious with him and at the same time utterly dismayed at what she had done. The last thing Julian needed was another wound. A woman's slap might not constitute much of an injury compared to what he had obviously been through but Anne felt terrible about it, all the same. She wanted to wrap her arms around him and tell him how sorry she was and knew she couldn't because he would totally misread the gesture.

"Just occasionally," he suggested brutally, "you might try reminding yourself that you're the one who came looking for me. If you don't like what you found, it's hardly my fault. Good night, Anne. Let me know if the sheikh shows up."

Anne watched in frozen silence as he stalked through the room toward a door he had tried earlier. The limp was very pronounced tonight and she knew his leg must be hurting him. Too much sitting still in a car and on the plane. But his broad shoulders were arrogantly straight, and there was more than enough dangerous male temperament in Julian to keep Anne very still until he had slammed the door shut behind him.

On the other side of the door Julian flipped on a wall switch and grimly surveyed the bedroom that adjoined Anne's fantasy tent. At least this room had been done in a more sensible style. He didn't much care for the early Western film look but he was relieved that he wouldn't have to put up with a bunch of filmy drapes over the bed. Feminine nonsense.

He might have been willing to tolerate the netting, of course, if it had meant he could have shared a bed with Anne. He was willing to be reasonable in some area. If she liked the drapes he would have put up with them to please her.

He'd have put up with a lot if it meant coaxing her into bed with him. Idly he fingered the still-stinging side of his jaw. Anne probably didn't realize how close to the edge she'd walked when she gave in to that burst of fury. It would have been very easy for him to have taken the angry passion in her and translated it into another, more sensual kind. God, he wanted her. His body was still taut with the heavy hunger.

Disgustedly he tossed his suitcase down on the bed and sat down to take off his worn leather boots. His leg was hurting him. It had stiffened up during the long day. Rummaging around in his case he discovered that Anne had packed her bottle of aspirin in with his overnight things. He sat staring at the little bottle, absorbing the implications of her thoughtfulness. Then he unscrewed the lid. Gulping down two or three of the white tablets he went in search of a glass of water.

The bathroom he found opening off his room was obviously meant to be shared with the occupant of the sheikh's tent. Mirrors lined every wall and the ceiling. Three steps led up to the huge oval red enamel tub. The rest of the fixtures were also in red, and the faucets were in a heavily scrolled brass. Huge bath sheets designed in a vaguely Oriental motif hung from the towel racks and a thick white carpet cushioned his bare feet.

Anne was going to love it, Julian decided in gathering irritation. He found a glass, filled it with water and downed the aspirin. On the other side of the wall he could hear Anne moving about in the sheikh's bedroom. Wait until she found out he would be sharing the bathroom with her. Maybe he'd time it so that he "accidentally" walked in on her when she was in the bath. Serve her right. Besides, he'd enjoy seeing her covered in nothing but soap bubbles.

Julian's annoyance grew as he undressed and fell into the rough-hewn bed. After reaching out to turn off the bedside lamp, he folded his arms behind his head and considered his relationship with the woman in the room next door.

She had a lot of audacity to think that she could just walk into his life and turn it upside down. The way she was leading him around—as if he were a bull with a ring in his nose—made him want to shake her. Who did she think she was, he wondered violently.

She'd had no right to turn up at the cabin the way she did. No right to see him when he was in the grip of that blasted fever. He couldn't figure out why she hadn't fled in disgust as soon as the roads were cleared. Whatever attraction he'd held for her must have suffered considerably when she found herself having to deal with the effects of that fever.

She'd seen the scars on his body, witnessed the way he limped and she knew how exhausted the illness had left him. He was definitely not the man he'd been when he left her six months ago. And he hadn't wanted to have her see him until he'd restored himself to some degree.

Julian remembered all the dark nights when he'd wondered if he would ever recover to the point where he felt confident enough to go in search of Anne Silver. Then she had disrupted everything by showing up in his life, long before he was ready for her.

He knew he'd been savagely short-tempered on occasion during the past few days. He'd been furious with her for seeing him in his weakened condition. But she'd tolerated the outbursts of temper. And she still refused to admit that she'd spent that first night in his arms.

Maybe she felt she had to have his help on this dumb project, Julian rationalized. Perhaps she'd put up with his illness and his temper because she couldn't think of anyone else who could assist her.

But Anne hadn't merely tolerated his illness. She'd offered comfort and compassion and a tenderness he'd never experienced before from any woman. Fleeting images of how she'd drained the unbearable heat from his body with wet sheets and then warmed him again when the chills had control came and went in his head. He couldn't remember details, had only hazy, dreamlike memories of those long hours when he'd been at the mercy of the raging fever, but he had been aware of the soothing voice and the comforting touch of her hand and Julian knew he'd never forget those images.

He could have chalked them up to feminine pity except for the fact that Anne didn't treat him as though she pitied him. She was still wary of him, still snapped back at him when she'd had enough of his uncertain temper and she still refused to admit to that night of passion. She was afraid to admit to her own surrender, Julian knew. Afraid to admit to his power over her.

No, she didn't pity him, he decided with some satisfaction. His hand moved to touch the side of his face where she had struck him so fiercely. A little hellcat, he thought with a wry twist of his mouth. Women who packed that much feminine outrage into a slap weren't feeling a lot of excess pity for their victim!

Julian turned on his side, automatically reaching down to massage his aching thigh. He didn't understand why she had tended him with such gentleness and why she hadn't found his weakness and his scars revolting, but he was sure now that she hadn't acted out of pity. He was instinctively certain, too, that she was nervous of his sensual power over her. Furthermore, she did need his help and protection while she carried out this scheme of Mike's.

He didn't understand her or what she felt for him, Julian realized as he drifted off to sleep, but he was beginning to think that maybe everything hadn't been ruined by her unexpected reappearance in his life.

Perhaps he had recovered more than he realized, because he was increasingly aware of the fact that he wasn't going to let Anne walk out of his life again now that he had her. He could handle his little hellcat. The knowledge felt good. For the first time in a long while his sleep was untroubled by dreams of a ghost woman.

Anne was not so lucky.

She explored the bedroom after Julian walked out, delighting in the unabashed ornateness of the tent scene. When eventually she discovered the red, white and brass bathroom she made a mental note to remember every detail for Lucy. They had made a joke out of the anticipation over the bedrooms because Miss Creswell had told Lucy to expect a treat. When Lucy and Anne had decided to switch places so that Lucy could stay with Michael, her future sister-in-law had begged for a full report.

"You know we don't allow ourselves to get that tacky here in Boston," Lucy had said with a grin. "I was really looking forward to indulging myself out there in California. Now I may never have another opportunity to experience West Coast decadence."

But some of the pleasure had gone out of her exploration, Anne realized. That last confrontation with Julian had squelched her sense of humor. Damn the man! Why couldn't he stop using his claws on her whenever she got too close? Tonight he'd taken one too many swipes, and this time she'd really lost her temper. She'd half expected him to slap her back, but instead he'd simply stalked out of the room. She hadn't been able to read the expression in those tawny-brown eyes, but she'd sensed the tight control he'd been exerting over himself.

Anne tried to put the unpleasant scene out of her mind as she crawled beneath the gossamer veils. Positioning herself in the exact center of the round bed, she reached out to carefully arrange the frothy drapery.

"I should get a camera and take a picture of myself in this thing," she muttered as she switched off the lamp. "When I'm very, very old I can take it out and show it to all my friends at the health farm. Tell them this is how I spent my younger days." It was a cinch that if she didn't make any more progress with Julian this fantasy bed was probably about as exciting as her night life was going to get. The thought depressed her.

SHE NEVER REALLY KNEW what it was that awakened her. Anne was aware of a chill in the room when she stirred drowsily several hours later. There was no reason on earth she should be so cold, she thought. Not when the thick down quilts were piled on top of her the way they were.

Maybe there was a thermostat on the wall. This huge old place had everything else, it probably had central heating. Anne twisted in the tousled sheets, reluctant to leave the comfort of the bed, but knowing that she was going to be uncomfortably cold unless she arose and found the heat.

If her room was so chilled, Julian's probably was also. That thought goaded her into sitting up in bed. The last thing he needed was to be exposed to too much cold. Anne opened her eyes and reached for the transparent bed veil.

And then she saw the figure standing at the foot of the bed.

The scream seemed to be locked in her throat. Anne's fingers clenched in the fine fabric of the veil. Her heart began to pound with fear and she told herself she was dreaming. There was no other explanation.

Dreams like this went away, she thought frantically. All she had to do was open her eyes. But her eyes *were* open. She was awake. She could feel the tissue-thin drape in her hand, was aware of the cold in the room, felt the light weight of the quilt on her legs. Dear heaven, she was awake!

Frozen in horror she tried to focus all her energy on allowing the scream to escape. Julian was in the next room. He would hear her. There was no doubt at all in her mind that if she could just yell for Julian he would save her.

As if she sensed that Anne was about to summon aid the woman at the foot of the bed, and it was a female, Anne realized vaguely, even though she was dressed in a man's riding costume, shook her head. There was a pleading expression on the pale features. Anne realized that she could see the wall behind the apparition even as she looked at her. She was able to see right through the figure.

The shock of that realization finally freed her vocal cords.

"Julian!"

The ghostly figure held out a hand in demand or appeal. Anne could not be sure which. But already the phantom woman was fading. A split second later, just as Julian flung open the door between the two bedrooms, the wraith disappeared completely.

"Anne, what the hell...?"

She struggled frantically to get through the bed veil. "Julian, oh, Julian, I've never seen anything like it. I must have been dreaming, but I *wasn't*. Julian, I... I...." She couldn't speak coherently and the stupid bed drape seemed to be deliberately impeding her escape.

"Take it easy, Anne," Julian soothed as he reached out and tore the veil aside. "What's going on? Why the scream?"

She threw herself into his arms, clutching at his

solid form with every bit of strength she possessed. A part of her realized that he was naked except for a pair of jockey shorts, but she was in no shape to concern herself with what he was or was not wearing.

"Julian, there was a woman. I could see right through her. She was standing at the foot of the bed and she...she...."

"Easy, honey, take it easy." His hand stroked her hair while she buried her face against his bare shoulder. Sitting on the rounded edge of the bed, Julian gathered her close, holding her on his lap and murmuring calming words.

"It was incredible, Julian," Anne whispered. "I've never...never had a dream quite that real."

"That's all it was, Anne. Just a dream." Julian wrapped her a little closer, pulling her more firmly into the warmth of his body. "Just a dream. Don't you think I know what it's like to have ghost women invade your dreams? Believe me, I'm an expert."

"But, Julian, she was there. Holding out her hand to me as if she wanted my help. I think she was wearing riding clothes. Old-fashioned, Spanish-style riding gear. But it looked like a man's outfit. You've seen those pictures of the tight black pants and white shirts with the little jackets...."

"I've seen plenty of them and that's probably why you dreamed that your visitor was wearing an outfit like that. One too many films of early California."

"But the figure in the dream was a woman. Wouldn't you think I'd have her in one of those beautiful, lacy gowns from the last century? Maybe a mantilla in her hair or something? I mean, why did I have her dressed like a man?"

Julian chuckled softly. "There could be some extremely complicated psychological reason for that," he pointed out gently.

"Uh-huh. Something along the lines of my subcon-

scious trying to project her in men's clothing because
even in my dreams I don't approve of the limitations
placed on women back in Carlota's time? Maybe I
tried to dress her in men's clothing because I wanted
her to have the freedom of a man. Not a bad piece of
analysis, Julian. Where in the world did you pick up
dream analysis techniques?''

Julian's mouth crooked at the sharp note in her
words. It was better than the panic that had been
there a moment ago. "I've told you, honey. I've had a
hell of a lot of experience in the subject. There were
times in my dreams when you seemed so real I
thought I could reach out and take hold of you.''

She stirred against his chest. "Really? What did you
plan to do to me after you had me?''

Julian looked down at her, studying her unexpectedly vulnerable expression in the shadows. "Well,
there were times when I thought I might beat you.''

"Thanks a lot!''

"Ah, but you deserved it,'' he assured her softly,
not entirely humorous now as he remembered just
how highly charged his emotions had been during
those dreams. "You showed up just when I seemed to
need you the most but you were always just out of
reach. It was frustrating beyond belief. I thought you
were going to drive me crazy and then, after a while, I
realized you were an indicator of the status of my
sanity. Whenever I saw you I knew I was hallucinating. When all I could see was jungle, I knew I was
seeing reality.''

She lifted her arms around his neck, her gaze wide
and intently serious. "Julian, what happened after
you went back to the island? Please tell me.''

"Not tonight, Anne. You've had enough of a nightmare for one evening. Think you can go back to sleep
now?''

"Are you ever going to tell me?''

"About what happened on that island? I doubt it," he said flatly. He felt her stiffen. "It's over, Anne. The best thing to do with nightmares is put them behind you and forget them."

"But you haven't forgotten. You remember every time your leg hurts or you come down with that fever. In fact, you probably remember the nightmare every time you look at me," she said with sudden, sad perception. "Oh, Julian, I never meant to do that to you. I don't want you to think of pain whenever you're around me. I should never have come looking for you."

"It's too late to have any second thoughts," he told her quietly. "You did come looking and regardless of what you intended, the result is what we both have to deal with."

"Meaning I've dragged the lion out of his lair and I have no one to blame but myself if I can't control matters?" she managed wryly.

"Is that how you think of me?" He was startled. "A lion?"

"I have a very vivid imagination," she explained apologetically. "Although, until tonight I had no idea just how vivid it could get!"

"The dream really shook you, didn't it?" Soothingly Julian began massaging Anne's nape. He liked that part of her, he realized. She was vulnerable there. Soft and vulnerable. And she seemed to respond when he stroked her like this.

"I've never had a nightmare quite that real, Julian." She leaned her head against his shoulder again, nestling into his warmth.

Julian found himself wondering at the unfamiliar sensations her trusting closeness was causing. Considering how badly he had wanted to make love to her earlier tonight it amazed him that he could be so content just to soothe her fears and cuddle her now.

She was really very vulnerable at this moment, he
thought. He could easily lay her back against the
pillows, talk to her a little longer until she was completely relaxed again and then gradually let his gentling touch grow increasingly sensual. He could have
her in the palm of his hand with very little effort. It
would be so simple now to make her admit to the passion that he had been able to draw from her the other
evening. If he handled her right he could spend the
rest of the night in bed with Anne making slow, overwhelming love to her. By morning she would be
unable to deny his power to make her respond.

But even as he told himself how assured the passionate victory was, Julian realized he wasn't going to
pursue it. Another desire in him was equally strong
tonight—stronger, in fact. He wanted to offer comfort
and reassurance and feel her respond to his gentling
touch rather than to his passion.

It was an odd need, unlike the straightforward, uncompromising desire he had allowed himself to experience in the past around Anne. Six months ago the
desire had been dominant. Whatever else he had felt
for her was easily buried beneath the relatively safe,
understandable, physical attraction. He had wanted
her from the moment he saw her, and he had told
himself that given time and opportunity he could
make her want him.

But both time and opportunity had been denied
him. He had returned from that godforsaken island
knowing he was in no condition to pursue and seduce
a woman like Anne Silver. She was a strong woman
and his instincts told him she would respond only to
a strong male. He needed time to recover at least some
of the easy masculine power he had once wielded so
casually.

Anne had shredded his plans and intentions when
she had showed up in the middle of the night asking

for help. The fact that he had been able to seduce her even though he had been on the verge of succumbing to the fever had restored a large chunk of his self-assurance, at least on the physical level.

By rights he should be pursuing that avenue of control. Instead he was taking a strange pleasure in being a source of comfort. Julian couldn't recall ever having offered a woman this kind of gentle reassurance. He couldn't recall a woman ever having asked for it. But, then, his relationships with the female of the species had always been a bit limited in scope.

Perhaps that was why Anne had gotten under his skin. Something in her had demanded more than simple passion from him and he had found himself wary of providing it. He wasn't even sure he had it within himself to give.

Tonight he began to wonder if he might have underestimated himself. Because tonight he was discovering that he did, indeed, have something other than desire to offer to Anne.

And judging by the way she was drifting off to sleep in his arms Julian could only assume that she needed what he was trying to give. It was a curiously satisfying realization.

6

ANNE CAME AWAKE THE NEXT MORNING with a gradual awareness of the fact that she was not alone in the theatrical bed. Julian's arm lay across her breasts and his heavy leg pinned her with unconscious ease. She allowed herself to savor the comforting warmth of him for a full minute before she opened her eyes and turned her head on the pillow.

It was a small shock to find herself confronting Julian's fully alert tawny gaze. Instantly Anne's focus moved to his shoulder in confusion.

"It's about time you woke up," Julian said equably. "We've got company."

"Company!"

"Ummm. Probably the housekeeper. I heard the car drive up a few minutes ago. Someone came into the house and headed toward the kitchen. We probably ought to go downstairs and introduce ourselves."

"The ever-alert secret agent," Anne grumbled, trying to ease out from under Julian's weight. "I didn't hear a thing." Very carefully she avoided meeting his eyes. "What are you doing here in my bed?" she went on uncertainly. "The last thing I remember you were patting my hand and telling me not to fret about ghosts."

He blinked with catlike interest. "The last thing you remember?"

"Well, yes. I had that horrid nightmare and you came running...."

"After you screamed bloody murder," he pointed out virtuously.

Anne grimaced. "I suppose I did. She shook me up a bit appearing at the foot of the bed like that."

"You don't really think you saw Carlota, do you?"

"Don't look so concerned for my mental health," Anne muttered. "I know it was a nightmare. That's not the point. The point is, what are you doing here in my bed? You should have gone back to your own room after...after...." Her voice trailed off.

"After cuddling you until you went back to sleep?" Julian yawned magnificently. "Yeah, I probably should have. But it didn't seem right to just abandon you after all that passionate lovemaking. Besides, it was cold, and a little shared body heat seemed like a good idea at the time."

"What passionate lovemaking?" Anne blazed, sitting straight up in bed and glaring down at him.

Julian looked honestly astonished. "Don't you remember? I was busy soothing you and trying to coax you back to sleep and all of a sudden you were dragging me down into the sheets and making very interesting love to me. Maybe it had something to do with having seen Carlota's ghost. Perhaps she inspired you. After all, from what you've told me the lady was quite a little wanton—"

He got no further. Anne seized the pillow and shoved it briskly down over his face, cutting off the taunting grin and the teasing words. "That's enough out of you, Julian Aries. I know perfectly well that I went straight off to sleep last night. Don't try making me believe that anything else happened."

"Muumph," he growled.

Whatever Julian was trying to say through the thickness of the down-filled pillow was drowned out by the knock that sounded on Anne's bedroom door.

"Good morning, Miss Melton," a bright voice sang out as a middle-aged woman wearing huge round glasses and a pair of very tight jeans pushed open the door and stood poised on the threshold. "I saw your

car in the drive. I'm Prue Gibson, by the way. I take
care of this place for Crazy Creswell. Thought you
might like a cup of coffee.... Oh, my goodness. I guess
I should have brought two cups up, hmmm?''

Her inquiring blue eyes went to Julian who was re-
moving the pillow from his face. For a moment the
two stared at each other, and then Julian smiled with
a graciousness that startled Anne. She'd never had occasion to see Julian making an effort to be polite and
charming. She was stunned to discover that he could
summon such casual aplomb under the embarrassing
circumstances.

"Good morning, Prue. I'm Julian Aries. And, as
you've already guessed, this lady with the startled
look on her face is Anne Melton. Miss Creswell's
niece and my fiancée. She's going to supervise the
ghost hunters for her aunt and I came along for the
free vacation. And a little honeymoon practice.''

Glibly Julian used Anne's assumed name and the
story she and Lucy had concocted. Miss Creswell had
told the housekeeper and Craven to expect a "Miss
Melton." She hadn't given Lucy's first name, so all
Anne had to change was the last. She'd been practic-
ing the switch silently for several days but Julian had
had very little time to become familiar with the roles.
It was a sign of his professionalism that he slipped
into the cover story as easily as a sword into a sheath,
Anne thought with an inner sigh. It was a little scary.

"Well—" Prue Gibson nodded amiably "—pleased
to meet you both. I see you've settled in nicely," she
added with a grin. "I'll just buzz back downstairs and
set an extra place at breakfast. You two come down
when you're ready." She closed the door behind her
with a brisk slam.

Anne flopped back against the pillows, a disgusted
expression shaping her mouth. "So much for preserv-
ing a little privacy and decorum!''

"Lucky we thought of the fiancé pose for me, hmmm? It would have been a little difficult to explain that you were in bed with the insane nephew formerly housed in the basement."

"Go take your shower," Anne ordered, "before I decide to find out if there are any sharks down there in that cove beneath the window."

"You're thinking of using me as the shark bait?"

"You've got it."

He gave her a persuasive, slightly hurt look. "Are you really so upset about what happened last night?"

"Nothing happened last night!" Anne hurled the pillow at him. Julian sidestepped it lazily, letting the soft missile strike the bathroom door. He might not ever regain the full power and speed he'd once had, Anne decided wryly, but there was no doubt that, even after what he'd been through, Julian's reflexes were faster than those of a lot of men who had never been injured or stricken with unnamed jungle fevers.

"Far be it from me to contradict a lady," he murmured. He moved forward, leaning down to cup her face in two strong hands. "If you want to pretend that nothing occurred...." He finished the words against her mouth, kissing her with warm, male satisfaction.

Anne's body melted beneath the gentle heat, her mouth opening to receive him without any conscious thought on her part. She felt his fingers teasing lightly at her nape and knew the extent of her own vulnerability around this man. But there was something new in this enveloping caress, a softness that was unfamiliar in Julian. Anne realized she found it utterly enthralling.

"Nothing happened?" he taunted lightly, flicking his tongue intimately into her ear.

"Julian, I recall perfectly well what occurred last night," Anne shot back as repressively as she could manage. "And I do not want to hear another word on the subject."

"Hmmm. A pity. Well—" he shrugged and released her, heading toward his door "—I can play the gentleman on occasion." His hand was on the doorknob. "Oh, one more thing. I take it our new friend Prue Gibson thinks everything is straight and aboveboard?"

Anne nodded, confused by the way he'd halted the kiss so easily. "She believes the ghost hunters are just what they say they are and that I'm here merely to represent Miss Creswell in the matter. I gather she thinks Miss Creswell is a little nutty. What did she call her? Crazy Creswell?"

"Probably because she's into the psychic phenomena bit. All right, that's what I wanted to know. I shall do my best to maintain your brilliant cover story," Julian said chuckling, finally closing the door behind him.

Anne stared at the door and then drew a deep breath, composing herself before she got out of the rumpled bed. Julian's sense of humor this morning was unnerving. Just as she'd never really been exposed to his charm, she'd also never had much opportunity to find out whether or not he had a real sense of humor. Every time they had been together it seemed the circumstances were too overlaid with urgency and emotion to allow for any exploration of the softer sides of his personality.

But it wasn't just his teasing humor this morning that was difficult to assimilate. There was also his gentle soothing in the dark hours of the night after she'd had that nightmare. Anne paused on the edge of the bed and allowed herself to dwell on that for a moment longer.

Whatever he claimed this morning, she knew very

well that there had been no lovemaking last night. Julian had held her and comforted her until she had gone to sleep. Then he had gone to sleep beside her. He had made no effort to take advantage of her emotional vulnerability last night.

All that left her with was a very big question. Why hadn't he taken advantage of the situation? She stood up and forced herself to consider the obvious answer. Perhaps he had simply been too exhausted!

That brought a rueful smile to her face as she went to the closet to find her robe. She would only be asking for trouble if she tried to read more into Julian's behavior than really existed. The man had been tired last night and he had every excuse in the world to be thoroughly worn out. He'd probably just gone to sleep without any further thought to the matter.

No, she must force herself not to read too much into Julian's actions. She would only be opening herself up to disillusion and hurt if she pretended that her wounded lion was beginning to gentle. For her own sake she had to remain extremely cautious.

Resolute in her decision, Anne flung open the door to the red-and-brass bathroom and stopped in her tracks. Julian was nonchalantly shaving in front of a steamed up mirror. And he wasn't even wearing the jockey shorts he'd had on earlier.

"Julian!"

He met her outraged eyes in the foggy mirror and grinned. "This wasn't exactly how I'd planned it, you know. I was intending to walk in on you. Preferably when you were sitting in a tub full of bubbles. Ah, well, the best-laid plans...."

He started to turn around and Anne hastily backed out of the room, slamming the door behind her. It was difficult enough dealing with Julian when he was wearing clothes. Confronting his unabashed nudity was quite another matter. There were definitely times when, for a woman, discretion was the better part of valor.

Prue Gibson was waiting for her two visitors downstairs. She surveyed them both with lively curiosity as they walked into the airy breakfast room, and immediately invited them to join her in the buffet breakfast she had prepared. Prue was clearly well into her second helping of fried potatoes and scrambled eggs. She was obviously not the deferential, retire-to-the kitchen, classic type of housekeeper, Anne thought in amusement. Always expect the unexpected in California, she reminded herself.

"So you two are going to entertain those weirdos for Miss Creswell, hmmm? Should be good for a laugh, if nothing else. I hope they're into séances and stuff. Always wanted to attend a real séance. When are the ghost hunters supposed to arrive?"

"This afternoon," Anne said calmly, helping herself to some eggs and a couple of pieces of whole-wheat toast. "What's your schedule, Prue? Are you here all day?"

"Miss Creswell phoned and asked me to stick around full-time during the days while everyone's here. My evenings are my own, though," she went on easily. "And if you don't mind my saying so, I've got better things to do than spend them here in this place."

"Afraid of ghosts?" Julian asked lightly as he poured himself a cup of coffee.

"What ghosts? That old tale of poor Carlota is pure garbage and everyone except the Creswell sisters know it." Prue Gibson laughed. "Nope, I said I've got better things to do with my evenings and I meant it. Just got married."

"Oh, congratulations," Anne said sincerely.

"We'll have to wait and see whether congratulations are in order. This is my third marriage. Harold's fourth. Nowadays it doesn't pay to jump to conclusions about how things will work out. Nice ring, though, don't you think?" She flashed the diamond solitaire with satisfaction.

"It's beautiful," Anne agreed politely.

"Harold's done okay in the stock market. In fact, he says he wants me to quit my job. I'm with one of those temporary help agencies, you know. Harold says we should go on a world cruise."

"Sounds like it would beat housekeeping," Julian observed, sipping his coffee slowly.

"I have a hunch it would," Prue said with a grin. "But when I took this assignment after the housekeeper retired, I promised the new owner I'd stay until she moved in and could line up someone permanently. This old place takes a lot of work on a daily basis. It can't stand empty very long or it really begins to look haunted."

"So you didn't work for my other aunt? The ex-movie actress who used to own this place?" Anne asked. She eyed Julian's cup of coffee with disapproval. So far he hadn't helped himself to any of the food.

"Nope. When she died, the housekeeper, who was getting on, retired. I understand the old actress was nice enough if you don't mind the eccentric type. She used to sleep in a different bedroom every night, I'm told. I see you two found one of the more interesting rooms last night. When are you planning on getting married?"

"We, uh, haven't set the date," Anne answered before Julian could open his mouth. She frowned across the table at her phony fiancé. "Aren't you going to have any breakfast?"

"I'm not hungry." He lifted one shoulder dismissingly.

"Well, you're going to eat," Anne declared firmly. She got to her feet and dished up a full plate of food. She had no intention of letting the man impede his own recovery by not eating properly.

"I said I wasn't hungry, Anne." There was an all-too-familiar thread of irritation in his soft growl.

Anne ignored the warning as she placed the plate in front of him. "You need the protein. Eat now and yell later."

Julian glanced down at the food and then looked over at an interested Prue. "Perhaps you can see why we haven't set the date for the wedding," he remarked meaningfully. "We have a few things to iron out between us first."

"You mean you aren't sure you can handle an assertive woman?" Prue shot back blandly.

"Is that what they call bossy, managing females these days? Assertive?"

"That's right," Anne assured him equably, watching in satisfaction as he began to fork up the eggs. "I'm assertive. Furthermore, I'm not the only female in this household who is. Prue, I'm sure, is on my side. Eat your toast."

"I appear to be outnumbered two to one." Julian picked up a slice of toast.

"Three to one." Anne smiled with an air of vast superiority. "Don't forget Carlota. From what I've read she was on the assertive side, too."

"That's right," Prue nodded pleasantly. "Legend has it, that little lady had a mind of her own and the guts to defy her husband. That took some doing back then."

It was Julian's turn to smile with cool arrogance. "Let's not forget what happened to her when she finally overasserted herself."

The comment effectively silenced the discussion on female assertiveness. Julian finished his eggs and toast with the air of a man who has just won a major victory.

It was after breakfast that Julian announced his intention to look over the house.

"Help yourself," Prue said airily. "I'm going to do some dusting and see that the rooms are ready for your ghost hunters." She started to step backward through the swing door into the kitchen with her hands full of dishes.

Anne recognized the routine and grinned. "How long did you work in a restaurant, Prue?"

The older woman looked surprised and then chuckled as she paused in the doorway. "Does it show?"

"Something about the way you back through that door reminds me of a part-time job I once had."

"No kidding. How long did you wait on tables?"

"Off and on for about four years. It was during the time I was in college."

"So what are you doing now? I mean, when you're not hosting a bunch of weirdos?"

Julian stepped in to answer before Anne could respond. "She's a research assistant at a fancy university back in the Midwest."

Anne was mildly surprised by the tone of his voice. She got the odd feeling that he didn't care for her job. "Don't look so impressed, Prue." She smiled. "I don't work in a lab or do any exotic testing. I have a background in librarianship and I know my way around a good research library. Mostly I work for a professor of history who's writing the ultimate book on the battles of the nineteenth century. Or thinks he is."

"Think anyone will ever read it if he gets it written?" Julian asked blandly.

"Oh, I'm sure he'll assign it to all his own classes. A small but guaranteed audience," Anne said with a chuckle. "The problem with history is not that people don't read it. It's that they don't seem to learn from it."

Prue laughed and disappeared into the kitchen. Julian continued to sit, staring thoughtfully at Anne.

"Do you really like that job?" he finally asked.

She wondered again at the faint hostility in his question. "It's a good job. Yes, I like it. It may lack some of the excitement and challenge your job has, but—"

"As my job *had*," he corrected quietly.

She frowned. "Julian, I know you're upset because you won't be going back to work at your old profession but don't expect me to sympathize. As far as I'm concerned you're well off out of it!"

"It paid well," he pointed out simply.

"So what?"

"So I could have offered—" He broke off abruptly, glowering down at his half-empty coffee cup. "Never mind. Unemployed males are occasionally moody."

"Is that right?" Anne grinned, tossing down her napkin. She leaned back in her chair, hooking her thumbs into her belt. "What next? Should we be making plans?"

Julian got to his feet. "Probably. That's why I thought I'd take a look around this place. I'm going to see what kind of security the house already has."

"Why?"

He gave her a mockingly patient look. "First, because if I know what kinds of locks and other security arrangements have already been made, I'll know what to expect if and when Craven and his bunch come back to carry out the burglary. And second, because I know a little bit about security in general. Supposedly this is the sort of expertise you came looking for when you came knocking on my door."

Anne lifted her chin. "You don't have to snap at me."

He closed his eyes in silent disgust. "I was not snapping at you. Not that you don't deserve it. Kindly

Harlequin Temptation™

Have you ever thought
you were in love
with one man...only
to feel attracted to another?

do not treat me as though I were a small boy at the breakfast table again, Anne."

"You need your food," she retorted stubbornly.

Julian lifted one sardonic brow. "I'm well aware of my own needs. And I'm capable of going after whatever it takes to fulfill them." With that he turned and stalked out of the breakfast room.

Anne sighed and decided that what she needed was a long walk on the beach. Julian's uncertain temper was very wearing at times. Determinedly she went into the huge kitchen to find Prue and ask for some advice on descending the cliff to the rocky beach.

Twenty minutes later Julian stood at an upstairs window and watched broodingly as Anne picked her way down the little-used path to the cove below the old house. She was moving carefully, choosing her route cautiously, and he guessed that the footing was uncertain. When she got back he'd issue a few well-chosen words of warning on negotiating the cliff path. Not that she'd thank him, Julian decided grimly. The lady was stubborn, arrogant and definitely self-assertive. She was also soft and sweet and deliciously vulnerable in bed. The combination was captivating.

Telling himself he had work to do, Julian turned away from the window and went to examine the lock on her bedroom door. Anne might be here because she was determined to carry out her brother's plan. Julian, however, knew that he was here, not because of Michael Silver, but to protect Anne. If Craven really was a crook, the first order of importance would be to keep an eye on the assertive little female who had concocted the situation in which Julian found himself. And he'd do it whether or not she appreciated his efforts.

Not liking the fact that Anne's hall door could be opened with a key from the outside, he took a few minutes to jimmy the mechanism so that it could no longer be unlocked from the hall, only from the bedroom. The task was child's play for him. He certainly owed the government for having provided him with an unusual and probably highly unmarketable set of job skills, Julian thought sourly. Anne was probably only impressed by those in academic careers.

When Craven and his small team arrived in a car three hours later, one of the first things Anne noticed was that two of the trio were very much academic types. For some reason she was surprised. None of the three looked at all as she had imagined.

"Thomas Craven," the portly, genial man announced as Anne opened the door. "I believe I and my friends are expected?" He smiled a gentle, ingratiating smile and fussed a bit with the wire-rimmed glasses that were perched on his nose. Craven was in his fifties, Anne knew, but she hadn't realized he would look quite so much like the scholarly professor of history for whom she worked. Balding, with friendly gray eyes and a fastidiously maintained mustache, Craven could have blended in with the academic crowd of any campus.

"Please come in, Mr. Craven. I'm Anne Melton," Anne said pleasantly, having practiced using Lucy's last name. "Did my aunt warn you I'd be representing her?"

"Of course, of course. Poor Miss Creswell. I understand she's most upset about the presence in the house. No need to be so nervous about those who have gone beyond. I have yet to uncover an instance where a presence has actually caused any physical harm to the inhabitants of a house. But I certainly understand how unsettling it can be to have an astral entity about the place." He turned to gesture to the two people standing on the steps behind him. "This is Sara. Sara is a sensitive."

"A sensitive what?" Anne asked blankly. She was

concentrating intently on the young woman in front of her. Sara was an ethereal beauty. Long blond hair, parted in the middle and falling to her waist, framed delicate, translucent features and a pair of dream-filled green eyes. Everything about the woman was as exquisite as fine crystal. She looked as if she'd shatter if someone shook her hand with too much force. Even as Anne asked her question, Sara was focusing on a silent Julian who stood waiting to one side.

"A sensitive is someone who has the ability to tune in to a presence, Miss Melton," Craven explained easily. "Sara has been gifted with a special kind of awareness. She's the one in our group who will actually be able to detect the presence, if there is one, and perhaps, if we're exceedingly lucky, communicate with it."

"How do you do, Sara," Anne managed politely. It didn't take any great sensitivity to see that Sara wasn't particularly interested in the formalities. "I didn't catch your last name."

"I have no last name," the young woman told her in a small, soft voice. "I'm just Sara."

"Oh."

"And I'm Dan Hargraves." The handsome man in his early thirties who stepped around Sara to offer his hand was refreshingly casual and open. "I'm Mr. Craven's assistant. I get to do all the research and keep all the notes. Glorified secretary, I'm afraid."

"I know the feeling," Anne said impulsively, responding to his easy manner before stopping to think. "I'm a research assistant myself. And there are times when I could have used a good secretarial course."

He grinned down at her as he shook her hand, his hazel eyes gleaming faintly. His hair was a light sandy brown, worn stylishly long. He was dressed more casually than the other two and there was a breezy charm about him that was quite attractive.

Especially when it was contrasted with the dark, saturnine presence of Julian, who was still standing quietly, waiting for the introductions. Anne hastily made them.

"My fiancé, Julian Aries," she said quickly, nodding toward him. Privately she was rather relieved not to stumble over the word fiancé. "He's, uh, taking a couple of days of vacation."

"Really?" Thomas Craven eyed him interestedly. "And just what is your line of work, Julian?"

"My fiancée was being polite when she said I was taking a vacation," Julian replied dryly, slanting a glance at Anne. "Actually, I'm unemployed at the moment. Want some help with the luggage?" He started out the door, not waiting for an answer. Dan Hargraves went to assist him.

"Are there just the two of you staying here, Miss Melton?" Craven asked politely as he stepped into the foyer.

"Just Julian and I and the housekeeper, Prue, who is only here during the days. You'll meet her shortly. She's out doing the grocery shopping. Please call me Anne, by the way." Leading the way toward the staircase, she went on chattily, "The bedrooms are a little odd but rather interesting."

"Fascinating," Thomas Craven observed as he and Sara followed Anne up the staircase. "Your aunt has inherited some excellent art, Anne."

"Oh, you mean the Ballards and the Renfrews?" Anne said easily, glancing at the watercolors that lined the staircase. "Yes, they are rather nice if you like that sort of thing. I've never been too fond of them, myself."

"Nevertheless, they're worth a fortune," Craven murmured, pausing to examine one in more detail.

"Ballard and Renfrew were friends of my other aunt. The one who originally bought this house. She was something of a patron to them when they were both young and struggling, I believe. They repaid her by giving her several pictures."

"Interesting." Craven smiled blandly.

Sara kept silent. She appeared to be lost in thought as she climbed the stairs behind Craven and Anne. Probably busy detecting presences, Anne decided uncharitably. Or else deciding whether or not to go to the bother of acquiring fakes to hang on the wall in place of the Ballard and Renfrew paintings, when the originals got themselves mysteriously stolen. Anne made a mental note to tell Julian that Craven had already shown an interest in the artwork.

Later that evening after dinner Craven helped himself liberally to the bottle of port in the living room and explained the procedure he and his companions would use to first detect the presence, as he called Carlota, and then remove her permanently. He was an excellent conversationalist, at ease with his audience, and in spite of what she knew about him Anne found herself listening intently to his stories. It was difficult to believe this was the man her brother had been trying to trap. For the first time Anne began to wonder if Michael might have been mistaken. But Lucy had said he was so sure it was Craven who had tried to get rid of him.

Uneasily Anne tried to sort through her impressions of the three ghost hunters as they all sat talking after dinner. When eventually Craven excused himself to go to bed she was no closer to any certainties than she had been earlier. In fact, she admitted to herself, she was beginning to feel very confused. Other than that Sara was definitely a bit strange, these people were all rather nice!

"I'm really looking forward to this assignment," Dan said pleasantly as he followed Anne into the kitchen after Craven had retired. Prue had long since gone home, and Anne was cleaning up the cups and saucers that had been used for after-dinner coffee.

"Anything special about this one?" Anne asked politely as the kitchen door swung shut behind them. She wondered what Sara and Julian would find to talk about alone in the living room.

"Mainly that it's taking place here in California," he said with a chuckle. "I've always wanted to visit California. Did you get to spend much time here when you were a kid?"

"Uh, no, my aunt didn't relish having kids around," Anne hastily temporized.

"Too bad. Can't imagine anything nicer than spending summers on this coast. When I was younger I always had a secret longing to follow the sun and become a full-time surfer." He set down the load of saucers he had been carrying and peered out the kitchen window. "Is the ocean really just down below us?"

"Yes."

"Mind if I step out on the terrace for a few minutes? I'd like to take a look at that cove you mentioned."

"You won't be able to see much at night," Anne warned. "There's not enough of a moon to...." Her words trailed off as Dan smiled and opened the kitchen door.

Curious, she followed him out onto the old brick terrace. The wind off the ocean was chilly, carrying the scent of the sea and promising a storm. What moon there was had already been obscured by clouds.

"Exciting, isn't it?" Dan murmured, as he leaned against the terrace railing and stared out at the night-darkened ocean. "A man could get addicted to the sea at night."

"It looks rather dangerous to me," Anne said with consideration, moving to stand beside him. Earlier that day the surf hadn't appeared to be too rough except where it broke over the rocks of the cove. But now, beginning to run before a storm, the waves looked and sounded considerably more violent. "But, then, I grew up in the Midwest. I've never felt entirely comfortable around oceans. I suppose I prefer lakes." She chuckled.

Dan laughed softly, and somehow he had moved a little closer. "Life is more fun when there's an element of danger in it. Maybe that's why I'm working as Craven's assistant."

"Is it dangerous?"

"Oh, not really, but one definitely encounters some strange tales and happenings in this line of work. To tell you the truth, Anne, I never believed in ghosts until I took this job with Thomas Craven. He and Sara have convinced me there are some really odd things in this world. Things that can't be easily explained by modern science."

"It must be fascinating," Anne observed cautiously.

"It is. Someday I'll write a book about it. Might as well use all the research for something useful."

Anne felt herself smiling in the shadows. "I've had the same thought from time to time. I spend so much effort doing research for someone else, and then I don't have the satisfaction of using it myself."

"Frustrating, isn't it?"

For a long moment they stood silently gazing out at the endless expanse of sea and then, with obvious reluctance, Dan drew a deep breath and straightened away from the railing.

"I suppose I'd better be getting upstairs to that wild Cleopatra-style bedroom. It's been a long day." But he didn't move for another minute or two, studying Anne's face in what little light emanated from the kitchen. "Yes," he said quietly, as if to himself, "I'm really looking forward to this particular assignment. And not just because of the ocean. Good night, Anne."

Anne watched in silence as Dan stepped back inside
the house. A very nice man. Someone with whom she
had something in common, too. The door closed behind him, and she was left alone on the night-
shrouded terrace. It was very chilly and damp, and
she told herself she should go back inside. She was
about to do exactly that when Julian's voice came to
her from the far end of the terrace.

"It's called 'divide and conquer' and although it's
an old strategy it can be remarkably effective," he
drawled in a low voice that sounded as though it had
been roughened by the wind.

Startled, Anne swung around, searching for him in
the shadows. He stepped silently out of the patch of
blackness that had been created by a tall hedge. "Julian! I didn't hear you. Where's Sara?"

"Gone to bed. She said she was tired."

"She looks like someone who needs a lot of rest,"
Anne heard herself say caustically. "A bit on the delicate side, wouldn't you say?"

Julian shrugged. "Maybe she's encountered one too
many ghosts. That's not what I wanted to talk about,
Anne."

"What did you want to discuss? Your habit of spy-
ing on people from the shadows? How long have you
been standing there, Julian?"

"Long enough. Don't give Hargraves any encouragement, Anne. He'll take advantage of it."

Anne bristled. "Really? And what about dear Sara?
Will she take advantage of you?"

"If I let her, yes. Like I said, it's called 'divide and
conquer.' Hargraves and sweet Sara are professionals,
remember? Liars, thieves and possibly worse, if Mike
was right."

"But they all seem so *nice*," Anne protested unhappily.

"Hargraves wants you to think he's the nicest guy

to come along since Santa Claus. It's to his benefit to see that you're left with a really terrific impression of him. That way you wouldn't ever dream of connecting him with the robbery that's going to take place at some point in the future. All three of them are going to want us to think they're *nice*. I told you on the way out here that you're going to do this my way, Anne, remember? You're to follow my orders. And my first order is that you watch your step around Hargraves. Keep him at a distance. No more dreamy little midnight scenes on the terrace."

Anne felt her temper start to simmer. "You're being ridiculous."

"No, Anne. Ridiculous is what I'd be if I didn't make certain, right from the start, that you remember I'm the one giving the orders. Now go inside and go to bed. It's late and it's getting cold out here."

Anne blinked, a little shocked at the steel in his voice. Julian was not speaking out of annoyance or irritation. There wasn't even any of the familiar frustrated masculine temperament in his words. He was suddenly very hard and very professional and he meant to be obeyed.

As Anne walked back into the house, her head held defiantly high, she had a distinct feeling of apprehension, which had nothing at all to do with ghosts. It had everything to do with her sudden certainty that Julian Aries at work was going to be even more formidable than Julian Aries recovering from his wounds and his fever.

7

IT WAS THE WIND that woke Anne several hours later. At least, that's what she assumed caused her to stir within the confines of the tented bed. It was a howling, gusty wind that carried the driving rain in from the sea—a wind well suited to a haunting. Sleepily Anne wondered if Craven and company liked the added bit of atmosphere the storm provided.

She turned drowsily to punch up her pillow, and that's when she saw the figure standing at the foot of the round bed. Anne froze in cold shock, staring through the misty veil at the apparition.

"No," she whispered in stark denial. "No, please...."

"Did you think I'd let you sleep alone tonight?" The phantom moved in the thick shadows, coming toward her around the bed. "After witnessing that cute little scene with Hargraves out on the terrace?"

"Julian!"

"Tonight we're not going to play any games," he swore softly as he stood on the other side of the bed veil and methodically began to unclasp his belt and step out of his jeans. Anne could see the outline of his bare, hair-covered chest in the darkness.

"Julian, please. I don't know what you think you're doing, but I do know I don't want you here tonight." And it was the truth. She did not want this man until he came to her with love. Anne knew that now. But she wasn't at all certain she could deny him if he ignored her wishes. Her own love for him weakened her.

"I am here, Anne. This time I can promise you that in the morning you won't be able to pretend that nothing happened." He was out of the jeans now, pushing aside the gossamer netting of the bed veil.

Instinctively Anne edged back, her pulse beginning to throb as a mixture of intense emotions coursed through her.

"There's nowhere to run, lady. Not tonight. Not tomorrow. You haven't had a chance since you foolishly turned up on my doorstep." Julian came down on the bed reaching for her.

There was heat in him tonight, Anne thought dazedly as he touched her, but not the heat of fever. The tawny-brown eyes gleamed faintly in the unlighted room but not with the unnatural glow of illness. Tomorrow morning he would remember all too well the effect he had on her senses. Anne thought she knew him enough now to know that he would not only recall exactly what he could do to her, but he would use the information. If she succumbed to his aggressive passion tonight she would be handing him a weapon he could wield against her.

"Julian, you must know I'm not about to get involved with Dan." Anne lay still beneath the chaining grasp of his hand. Something told her that if she struggled he would respond by pinning her more firmly to the bed.

"I know that," he agreed. "And tomorrow morning you'll know it, too. You'll also know that there won't be any more professors of either English or history or any therapists from the physical-education department. In fact, after tonight there won't be anyone else for you except me."

Suddenly Anne became angry. "You're only doing this so that you can control me, aren't you?"

"The strange part is that for the past six months I wouldn't have guessed I could control you this way," he said huskily as he settled his heavy thigh over her lower body. "I told myself you needed someone stronger—that I would have to wait until I had fully recovered. I was too proud to face you until I knew for certain you wouldn't pity me or find me weak."

"Oh, Julian," she whispered, lifting her hand to touch the side of his hard face. "The one thing I have never felt for you is pity."

"I know that now. I think I knew it that first night. I seduced you that night at the cabin, didn't I? I carried you off to bed and made love to you until you were helpless in my arms. You surrendered that night and you knew it. It wasn't pity you were feeling. In fact you were a little afraid of just how completely you had surrendered, weren't you? That's why you denied everything the next morning." He lowered his head deliberately and grazed his lips along the line of her throat. When she trembled in reaction he muttered his sense of satisfaction. "Do you have any idea of how it made me feel to know that I had that kind of power over you? Even though I was on the verge of another attack of that fever?"

"Julian, I don't want it to be like this between us. I don't want you to make love to me because it gives you a feeling of... of power or control. It should mean something else—something more important."

He looked down into her pleading eyes and traced the line of her slightly parted lips with his thumb. "Honey, you don't know just how important it is to me to feel this sensation of power over you. You don't know how good it feels to know I can make you surrender completely. Believe me, after all these months of thinking I wasn't the same man you had been attracted to in the beginning, it was very, very satisfying to know I could still make you want me."

"You're so damned arrogant," she breathed helplessly. *And you know exactly how to disarm me,* she added silently. There was no way she could fight him to-night. Not after that small confession of his. It was incomprehensible to her that he could have believed she wouldn't be as attracted to him now as she had been six months ago. "And you're far too proud," she told him.

"But I can make you shimmer in my arms, can't I?"

"Only because...."

"Because?"

Anne sighed in surrender, her hands clinging to the solid planes of his shoulders. She couldn't tell him that she loved him. Not yet. Julian Aries wouldn't understand that emotion. He saw things in simpler, more fundamental terms. "Only because you're Julian."

He hesitated no longer. "Anne...!"

She felt his strong fingers on the buttons of her flannel gown and she cried out softly when he undid them all so that he could slip his hand inside.

"You're so soft," he murmured. "I dreamed of your softness—longed for it." His mouth moved hungrily from the base of her throat to the opening of the nightgown, seeking the budding tips of her breasts.

Anne felt herself being crushed back into the bedding. Dreamily she realized that the flannel gown had been removed completely and that Julian was exploring her body with bold wonder.

"Do you like my touch?" he demanded provocatively, trailing his fingers down her stomach to the dark mystery between her legs. "Do you, Anne?"

"You know the answer to that. Oh, Julian, *please*."

"I want to feel your hands on me, honey." His tongue moved tantalizingly over her nipple. He caught hold of her wrist and dragged her fingers along his side to his muscular hip. "Touch me, Anne. Let me know how much you want me."

She sensed the need in him and knew it was as great

as her own. Perhaps he did think in terms of power and control. Perhaps recovering that purely masculine arrogance was a necessary part of his recuperation. In any event it was all he had to offer her now and Anne knew she would take what she could get.

Slowly she traced the hard male outlines of his body, thrilling to his obvious response. Maybe he did have power over her she thought wonderingly, but she also had a certain amount over him. And it was an intoxicating kind of knowledge.

Gently she pushed against his shoulders until he allowed her to roll him over onto his back. And then she found the base of his throat with her lips.

"Anne—" Whatever he would have said next was lost in a thick male groan of rising hunger as she strung tiny kisses down to the flat masculine nipples.

When she carefully let him feel the edge of her teeth he shuddered violently, his palms moving down her back to the curve of her buttocks. As she worked her way lower, so did he. Anne felt his hand slide down to the flowing heat between her legs.

Her fingers closed delicately on the shaft of Julian's manhood, drawing a fierce, swallowed sound of need from him. And then he was probing the moistness of her, using her own warmth to smooth and lubricate the sensitized flesh between her thighs. Aching to give him back some of the passionate heat he was generating in her, Anne bent her head and brushed her lips intimately against him.

"My God, Anne, you'll drive me out of my mind." He uncoiled beneath her, pushing her back into the sheets again. "Out of my mind...." He trapped one budding nipple between his front teeth and tantalized his captive with incredible gentleness.

Julian's hand flattened on her stomach and then went lower. His mouth followed until Anne cried out and clenched her fingers in his hair.

The night and the storm flowed around them and through them, closing out all but the deep mysteries of passion. Julian made love with an uninhibited aggression that excited Anne beyond anything she had ever known. It turned her into a creature who both delighted and demanded. The scope of her own desire amazed her, and Julian's escalating response captured her senses.

When he finally moved to cover her body with his own, she pulled him to her with urgent little cries. He fed on the soft sounds, plunging his tongue forcefully between her lips a second before he filled her body with his uncompromising hardness.

"Julian, Julian," she gasped as he thrust completely into her. She was pinned beneath his weight, her legs forced widely apart so that she was totally vulnerable. Anne felt at once ravished and wanton—the one who is taken and the one who takes. She wrapped her lover tightly to her, sinking her small, white teeth delicately into the muscle of his shoulder as the driving rhythm of his lovemaking grew in intensity.

When the moment of utter release descended on her she clung to the man who had provided it, refusing to let go until he had joined her. She had the fierce satisfaction of hearing her name on his lips as he arched violently against her, and then the thick shadows enfolded them.

It was a long time before Julian stirred on her, uncoupling slowly, reluctantly, to roll to one side. Then he gathered her against him, his arm curved around her.

"Remember this the next time Hargraves turns on the charm," he rasped. "Remember that now you belong to me." Lazily he traced a circle around the tip of her breast. "You're the one who came looking for me, honey. And you're going to have to take what you found."

She raised herself on one elbow to gaze down at him. "You sound possessive," she whispered.

"I'm feeling possessive." His mouth curved with masculine content.

"Were you jealous of Dan?"

"Let's just say I'm taking steps to protect you from him."

"You were jealous," she accused softly.

Julian hesitated as if considering his words. "Hargraves is going to hold out all the bait I haven't got to offer."

"That's ridiculous!"

"Is it? He's going to show you how much you have in common, how similar your professional interests are, how charming and considerate he can be."

"He's involved with the people who tried to kill Michael. How could I possibly be attracted to him?"

"Tonight you were already questioning his involvement. All three of them were so *nice*, you said. Remember?"

"Well, they are. At least Craven and Dan are nice. I can't quite figure out that Sara. Isn't it a bit affected not to have a last name?"

"Goes with the image."

"I suppose. Julian, you don't have to worry that I'm going to forget the reason I'm here," Anne told him vehemently. "After all, I'm the one who set this up. It's my brother lying in that Boston hospital!"

"Honey, you're not used to dealing with real con artists. The nicer they are and the more charming they seem, the more you're going to question your own judgment."

"So you assaulted me tonight in an effort to remind me that you're in charge and I'm not to let myself get led astray by the opposition, right?" She flopped back on the pillow, pulling the comforter up to her chin and staring angrily up at the draped netting.

Julian turned on his side, regarding her with something between amusement and speculation. "Is that what you considered it? An assault?"

"You scared the daylights out of me by just appearing at the foot of the bed the way you did," she accused morosely. "At first I thought it was her...."

"Her?"

"The ghost I thought I saw last night. The one in my dream. I couldn't see you very well through this stupid veil."

"I'm sorry I frightened you." He bent his head to brush his mouth against her ear.

"But you're not sorry you assaulted me?" she challenged.

"No. In fact, I'm seriously thinking of doing it again," he teased.

Anne turned her head in astonishment. "You are?"

"Ummm. But first I want you to admit you do remember that first night at the cabin."

"Never," she declared loftily.

"Never is a long time. But not quite as long as the rest of tonight." He pushed his hand beneath the down-filled comforter and flattened his palm on her stomach. "There's no point denying it, honey. I know I carried you off to bed that night. I've gotten very good at telling the difference between reality and illusion lately."

Anne looked up at him from under her lashes. "Maybe I'm not quite so adept at it." And maybe that was the truth. How much of an illusion was she weaving for herself when she pictured a future of love with Julian Aries?

Then his hands were moving on her again, and she no longer cared about the difference between the real and the unreal. Only Julian's touch mattered.

WHEN ANNE AND JULIAN WALKED into the breakfast room the next morning it was to find that Thomas Craven had already preceded them. He was involved in a lively conversation with Prue Gibson, who was sparkling even more than usual under Craven's gentlemanly charm.

"Good morning, you two," Prue called out cheerfully, pouring coffee into two cups. "How did you sleep last night? That was quite a storm we had, wasn't it? I was just telling Thomas here that legend has it little Carlota was trying to make her escape on a night like last night."

"I've never quite understood why ghosts and storms go together," Thomas said genially as he sat back and sipped his coffee. "But there is a definite corelation. In many of the cases I've investigated the presences are felt most strongly during a severe storm. It will be interesting to see if Sara experienced any emanations last night."

"I expect ghosts and storms go together because people's imaginations seem to become more vivid under stormy conditions," Julian remarked coolly as he handed a cup of coffee to Anne and then helped himself.

"You sound like a skeptic, Julian." Thomas Craven smiled blandly. "Only to be expected. Most people are until they've actually experienced a presence or witnessed the results of one passing through. I myself used to scoff at the idea of ghosts, but in my line of work you quickly become convinced. I set out to disprove the legends and tales I had been collecting and found myself unable to ignore the evidence. But I still maintain a scientific approach to the matter, and in many of the cases I'm called in to investigate I wind up proving there is no presence. In other cases my friends and I have been able to provide tranquillity to homes that have been troubled."

Julian shrugged with evident disinterest. "Well, it's

Miss Creswell's money. If Anne's aunt wants to pay you to de-ghost her house that's her business.''

"Still," Dan Hargraves remarked from the doorway, "it must be a little galling for a man who is currently unemployed to see money being spent in such a frivolous fashion. Then again, I suppose you can afford to take the long-term view. After all, you're going to be marrying one of Miss Creswell's heirs, aren't you?''

The silence that followed the provocative insult was broken only by the sound of Anne choking on her coffee. She couldn't believe Dan had had the nerve to offer such a challenge to Julian Aries, even if he truly believed that Julian's motives were questionable. Dan had no way of knowing that the whole engagement was a farce, of course. He was reacting to the situation that had been presented, and Anne could only assume he was deliberately insulting Julian for a reason. She just couldn't imagine what the reason would be.

Neither, apparently, could anyone else in the room. Even Prue was momentarily silenced in astonishment. Craven looked pained. Anne was struggling to find words with which to smooth over the situation when Julian spoke.

He regarded Dan with laconic boredom, as if the younger man was a rather annoying rodent that had wandered into the house. "You can skip the not-so-subtle insults, Hargraves. Anne and I understand each other very well." His dark-gold eyes went to Anne's face, and only she saw the warning in those depths. "She knows, for example, just what holds our relationship together and it has nothing to do with money. Isn't that right, honey?''

Anne's temper flared. She knew he was deliberately setting a public seal on her. A seal that would accompany the very private one he had placed on her last night. The desire to tell him to go to hell was brought under control only with a great deal of difficulty. Instead she managed a smile while telegraphing her anger with her eyes.

"Oh, yes. Julian and I understand each other." But he didn't understand her. Not at all. And she was beginning to wonder if he ever would.

It was Sara, appearing in the doorway, who succeeded in dispelling the tension of the moment. Everyone at the breakfast table swung around as she made her entrance. And "entrance" Anne thought, was the right word. Pale, beautifully wan, a weightless smock of embroidered gauze drifting around her slender frame, Sara definitely looked a little ghostly herself this morning. The long blond hair had been brushed until it hung like a silken curtain around her shoulders, and it occurred to Anne that sweet Sara had taken a bit of time with her appearance. She wondered how much luck the blonde had with that fragile look.

"She's here, Thomas," Sara whispered. "I felt her presence last night. Oh, Thomas, she is in such agony. We must free her." Her voice broke on the last words and she rushed toward Craven. Thomas patted her with what seemed to Anne to be slightly more than a paternal touch.

"All right, Sara. All right, dear. Just calm yourself. Everything's going to be fine. Just fine."

Sara sniffed delicately, and a single, glistening tear appeared on her cheek. The woman really was overplaying her part, Anne decided, casting a wry glance at Julian. The glance became a glare as she realized Julian was staring at the other woman with fascinated concern.

"Did you actually see her, or were you only able to sense the presence?" Dan asked in a practical tone.

"Last night I could only feel her. She was there in

my room. I think she came looking for me because she knows I can communicate on some level with her. She's desperate. She's been confined so long now, trapped in this old house because it was built on the ruins of her home. She is a very sad creature."

"What's the next step?" Julian asked interestedly.

"We must establish a more definite contact," Craven explained. "Sara can only do that by going into a full-scale trance of sorts."

"A séance!" Prue exclaimed, looking delighted. "How exciting."

"Well, it's really not that much fun," Dan told her in mild amusement. "It can be very traumatic on occasions, and it always leaves Sara wiped out for most of a day."

"Still, it's the only way we can determine exactly what the presence requires in order to be freed," Craven said with a sigh.

Anne remembered the tale she had researched. "According to the legend, Carlota returns to look for something. Will we actually have to find it for her in order to get her out of the house?"

"Not necessarily. Usually in cases such as this one the presence has somehow become trapped in a loop."

"A loop?" Julian asked. "You mean like a program loop in a computer?"

"Not a bad analogy," Craven nodded, pleased. "That's exactly what it's like. In a program loop the machine gets stuck going from A to B and back again and can't escape to continue with the program. One has to go into the program itself and correct the flaw that has trapped the machine. Presences who died in sudden violence occasionally seem to be caught in that sort of trap—unable to break free of their earthly ties, but no longer a real part of this realm. Their despair is often the first sensation Sara feels. Somehow we have to break the loop cycle."

"When do we get to hold the séance?" Prue demanded.

"I think this afternoon," Craven announced, glancing at Sara to see if that was all right with her. "It doesn't always work the first time, however. It may be necessary to hold two or three of them in order to achieve an adequate level of communication."

"I see," Anne said briskly. "Well, eat hearty, Sara. You look as if you'll need the energy. You look a little run-down," she added too sweetly.

Julian tossed Anne a half-amused, half-rebuking glance but Anne just smiled quite brilliantly.

THE SÉANCE THAT AFTERNOON was not at all what Anne had expected. There were no artificial trappings, no crystal ball, no velvet-draped surroundings. The fog, which was beginning to roll in from the sea, did manage to provide a certain air of gloom, but that was it as far as lighting effects went. Craven had decreed that Sara use the living room.

"We can build a fire in the fireplace," he explained. "Sara often gets quite cold when she's in a trance. The added warmth can be very comforting to her."

Julian did not offer an opinion on the subject. He just went about building the fire with casual efficiency. Anne was idly noting that his leg didn't seem to be bothering him so much today in spite of the foggy chill outside, when she realized that she wasn't the only one watching Julian lay the fire. Sara's pale, haunting gaze was also on him as he knelt to set a match to the kindling. In fact, Anne decided in disgust, Sara had been paying a lot of attention to Julian.

"Thank you, Julian," the blonde murmured in her gentle voice. "I shall soon be very grateful for the added warmth. I get so cold sometimes...."

"Maybe you should try wearing a sweater and

slacks," Anne suggested, "instead of that little light-weight nightgown."

Sara gave her a reproachful glance. Julian, standing directly behind the blonde, sent Anne a warning glare. Anne ignored both.

"I have to feel free when I'm trying to communicate," Sara explained gently. "Wearing loose-fitting, light clothing helps me achieve that feeling."

"Well, now," Craven interrupted genially, "I think we're all set. Don't overexert yourself, Sara. Just go as far as you comfortably can. Let's see if we can even make contact."

"Do we all get to sit in a circle and hold hands?" Prue asked.

"I'm afraid that's an old charlatans' technique," Dan said chuckling. "Really not a necessary step at all. The fake psychics just wanted to make sure everyone's hands were occupied so that the people around the table wouldn't accidentally touch any of the rigged apparatus."

"Will we be able to see anything at all if Sara makes contact?" Anne inquired curiously.

"I'm afraid not. Only a true sensitive can see the presence and even sensitives often have to rely more on sensation rather than sight. Occasionally there will be a manifestation of noise but that's rare."

"How disappointing," Prue grumbled.

"If Sara does make contact, we'll be able to ask questions through her. That can be very interesting," Dan consoled the older woman lightly.

Craven decreed quiet as the group took their places in chairs near the fire. Sara sat on the floor in a lotus position facing the flames on the hearth.

Craven turned off the living-room lights, and Anne suddenly realized just how thick the late-afternoon fog had become. There was an eerie, gray, dimensionless feeling to the day, as if the strange old house were adrift in a sea of endless fog. Even the familiar noise of the surf seemed muted. Only the fire provided any note of warmth and light. Anne suddenly understood why Sara demanded it. A person could get so cold on a day like this. So very cold....

She shivered as silence fell on the room. Sara's eyes were closed and everyone else was watching the blonde. Anne thought seriously about getting up to change the thermostat setting, but for some reason it seemed like too much of an effort. And she didn't want to disrupt the mood of the quiet room. Not now.

It was almost unpleasantly cold in the room, Anne realized a few minutes later. Nothing had happened, but she had the strangest impression that someone had left a door open somewhere and that tendrils of fog had found their way into the living room.

Sara broke Anne's strange feeling of lethargy with a chant. The meaningless words disturbed something in the atmosphere. Anne moved restlessly, wishing the woman would shut up. She wanted to listen, pay closer attention to the flickering flames on the hearth. There was a message in those flames, a meaning. No, not in the flames—in front of the fire. The air in front of the fireplace seemed to shimmer faintly. Anne wished desperately that Sara would stop chanting. It was so annoying and it was disturbing whatever hovered in front of the fire. Then Sara spoke.

"We are here to help you, Carlota," Sara said in a singsong voice. "We only wish to help."

Instantly whatever had been there in front of the fireplace was gone. Almost at once Anne began to feel warmer. She shook her head in an attempt to clear it of the dazed, lethargic sensation and became aware of Julian's solid presence beside her. When she slanted him a glance out of the corner of her eye she saw him carefully watching Sara.

Craven sat with his eyes closed, his hands folded

over his portly stomach. Dan was also watching Sara, but he looked quite relaxed. Prue appeared vividly curious and was focusing intently on Sara. None of them seemed to have felt the earlier chill in the room, and none of them looked even slightly dazed. Maybe she was one of those people who could easily be hyp- notized, Anne told herself by way of explanation. But that didn't make any sense. The weird sensation had begun to occur before Sara had started in on her re- petitive chant. On the other hand, Anne decided grimly, perhaps she'd merely let her own imagination run away with her.

"Help you, Carlota. Help you. We only want to help you. Tell us...."

Sara's low, singsong voice began to bore Anne. She was wishing she'd thought to fix some coffee before starting the séance, when suddenly the blonde's tone changed.

"Yes," Sara whispered. "Yes. I can feel you Carlota. Just as I felt you last night."

Craven opened his eyes and sat forward, staring in- tently at his assistant. Dan Hargraves also took on an air of focused attention. Prue looked hopeful, and Ju- lian's expression didn't change at all.

This was utter nonsense, Anne thought disgust- edly. There was nothing else here in the room with them. Not now at any rate. But Sara was beginning to carry on some sort of odd conversation.

"I know you need help. Can you tell me what to do?"

Silence. Presumably, Anne decided, the ghost of Carlota was answering.

"Yes, Carlota. I understand that you search. But for what?"

Silence again.

"Peace, Carlota? Justice? I don't understand. What do you wish of us?"

Everyone remained very still during the next stretch of silence, and then Sara gave a startled cry. The flames on the hearth flared abruptly higher turning a brilliant shade of green. The fluorescent green gave way to vivid blue and finally burned silver.

Sara collapsed, falling forward so that the curtain of blond hair was flung like a cape around her. Dan was instantly on his feet, lifting her and settling her into a nearby chair. Craven looked concerned but not unduly worried.

"She'll be all right," he told the others. "Just give her a couple of minutes. Have you any brandy, Prue?"

"Right over there on the cart. I'll get it." The housekeeper hurried across the room and returned with a large dose of brandy in a glass and held it to Sara's lips. A moment later the blonde opened her eyes and smiled wanly up at Prue.

"Thank you," she murmured, accepting a few sips of brandy.

"Did you really see her?" Prue asked expectantly.

"Yes. The presence is a very strong one. She...she wants to be released."

"Did she say how that could be achieved?" Dan asked quietly.

"She says the truth must be told. She said something about the legend being a lie. A lie that trapped her here. If the truth is told to us, the living, she will finally be able to go beyond and join her lover."

"The woman has a one-track mind," Julian observed. "Even as a ghost all she can think about is running off with her lover. No wonder her husband strangled her."

"Julian!" Angered by the lack of sympathy, Anne turned on him. "You know nothing about the situation. I'm sure Carlota was very much in love and feeling very trapped in an arranged marriage. All she wanted was to be free."

"And that's the one thing she still seems to want," Dan said mildly. "When do we get the whole story, Sara?"

"It was my fault things ended when they did," Sara said apologetically. "I couldn't take the full force of her presence in one sitting. She recognized that and said she would return when I had rested and could call for her again. She'll tell us the tale and then she will be free."

"What did she look like?" Prue demanded, obviously enthralled with the whole business.

"Very beautiful. Black hair, dark eyes. Very aristocratic looking." Prue smiled.

Anne didn't know what made her ask the next question. It was as if she couldn't help herself. "What was she wearing, Sara?"

Sara looked momentarily taken aback. She recovered herself quickly, however. "A lovely gown of black lace. A wide, full skirt. Her shoulders were bare, I think. And there was some sort of hair ornament. A comb trimmed in silver, I believe. I'm sorry, I wasn't paying that much attention to her clothing."

"I'm not surprised. Must be quite an experience talking to a ghost," Anne said quietly. And then she thought of the woman she had seen in her dream the first night at the house.

The phantom had been very lovely with dark hair and dark eyes. But she hadn't been wearing a lace gown. She had been dressed in a man's riding clothes. It was understandable that Sara's description of Carlota was the expected one. It could have been drawn from a portrait or a film.

Why had her own imagination turned up a Carlota wearing riding gear?

8

JULIAN SAT DOWN WEARILY on the edge of the Western-style bed, slowly unbuttoned the blue work shirt he was wearing and wondered how Anne would go about telling him she wasn't going to sleep with him tonight.

He was prepared for the small confrontation. He'd seen it coming all afternoon. The speculative glances she'd given him when she thought he didn't notice, the restless uneasiness in her when he'd sat down beside her after dinner and the hint of defiance in her bearing when he'd quietly announced it was getting late.

She hadn't argued when he'd deliberately risen to his feet and then waited for her to precede him up the stairs. Saying a polite good-night to Craven and his friends, she had obediently walked to the staircase and along the corridor to her room. There she'd smiled very coolly and closed the door gently in his face. Julian had been forced to use the hall entrance to his bedroom rather than the connecting door from Anne's room.

He could hear her now, moving about in the sheikh's tent. He wondered sardonically what she would do if he simply opened the connecting door, walked into her room and climbed into bed. At the very least he'd get a display of outrage and defiance.

Little did she know he wasn't going to make matters difficult tonight. He'd made his point last night. And he'd been reasonably satisfied with the results today. Whenever Hargraves had tried to maneuver too close to Anne she had warily, if politely, sidestepped. The distance she had put between herself and Hargraves was carefully maintained, at least whenever Julian was in sight. Julian had been careful to be in sight most of the time.

By dinnertime Hargraves had stopped making a serious effort to approach Anne. He seemed to realize she wasn't going to encourage the process and that suited Julian just fine.

Julian told himself he had accomplished what he'd set out to accomplish last night when he'd invaded Anne's room. If she hadn't fully accepted his claim, at least she wasn't going to defy him or his rule.

He cocked his ankle over one knee and started to pry off the worn leather boot. The small effort made him wince as his upper leg protested. Damn that leg. How many more months was it going to act up under the slightest provocation?

He'd thought the thing was improving. The familiar ache had been considerably lessened this morning. But then the damp fog had rolled in off the sea to shroud the house, and by evening his thigh was beginning to throb again.

He should probably dig out that aspirin Anne had packed. Somehow it seemed almost too much effort to get up, walk across the room and find it in the suitcase. Julian sat on the edge of the bed and thought that what he really wanted tonight was to have Anne massage his leg.

The realization darkened his expression into one of fierce denial. The last thing he would do was ask Anne for a massage. She'd already witnessed enough of his various and assorted physical weaknesses. It was intolerable to even think of telling her he needed her gentle touch. He would not risk undoing the bonds he had placed on her last night, and if she lost respect for him that was exactly what would happen. No, he couldn't ask for her help. Not tonight.

But, oh hell, it would be so good to be able to lie down and let her soothe the ache in his leg. So very good. Memories of the way she had massaged away the pain in his neck and head when he'd been recovering from the fever returned to taunt him. All he had to do was open the door and ask.

No. He wasn't that weak. Disgustedly Julian finished undressing, out of long habit leaving on only his shorts. He found the bathroom unoccupied and brushed his teeth. A brief notion of taking a hot shower to see if that would help the ache in his leg went through his head, but somehow it all seemed like too much work. He did manage to dig out the aspirin, although he was skeptical about how much good it would do.

Julian was throwing back the Indian-patterned blankets and climbing into bed when the tentative knock came on the connecting door. *Oh, yeah. The confrontation.* Little did she know that with the way his leg was hurting he was in no mood to play the demanding lover.

"Hello, Anne," he managed in a nonchalant drawl as he opened the door. "Come to seduce me?"

"Hardly," she retorted with a ferocious little frown, as she made a determined effort not to let her eyes drop below his chin. "I wanted to talk to you, Julian."

"I'm always willing to talk to a woman when she's standing in front of me wearing a nightgown," he murmured, opening the door farther and stepping aside. She looked rather sweet in that soft-flannel gown, he decided, in spite of the frown. Her hair had been set free from the sleek knot in which she'd worn it most of the day, and now the autumn-colored stuff was falling in undisciplined curls around her shoulders. God, she looked good. And her gentle hands would feel so wonderful.

"Julian," she began, her chin lifting with an imperiousness that amused him, "I would like to get something straight between us." She walked stiffly into the room and turned to face him again.

Some of Julian's affectionate amusement faded. It was bad enough that he didn't even feel he could risk asking her to massage his leg. He didn't particularly want to hear that she didn't want to sleep with him, as well. He understood that she needed to assert herself a little, after what had happened the previous night, but he didn't want to listen to the entire speech.

"It's all right, Anne, you don't have to worry about tonight." With an unconscious gesture of weariness he rubbed his jaw, realized what he was doing and stopped immediately. "I think we got the main points out of the way last night, don't you?"

"I'm in no mood for your macho attitude. I won't have you thinking you can control me with sex."

"It never occurred to me that I could," he told her dryly.

"No? You've been awfully cool and sure of yourself today."

"Is there some reason I shouldn't be sure of myself?"

A slight flush stained her cheeks. "It's just that I . . . I don't want you to think that because you invade my room and make love to me you therefore have a whole new set of rights over me. Julian, I don't want to argue. I just want you to understand that—" She broke off, glaring at him intently. "What's wrong?"

"What could be wrong? I'm getting ready to go to bed and you're standing here giving me a lecture on sexual ethics. It wouldn't be so awkward, I suppose, if you weren't wearing a nightgown but since you have invaded my room dressed like that, what am I supposed to think?''

"Lie down," she ordered briskly.

He gave her a speculative, narrow look. "Why?"

"I'm going to massage that leg for you." She was already moving over to the bed and arranging the blankets.

"The leg is fine, thank you. Now don't you think you'd better get back to your own room before I start misreading your intentions?" he asked.

"My only intention is to massage that leg for you. Lie down, Julian. Humor me, okay?" She gave him a bleak smile.

"Anne, I don't .... Oh, hell. If it will pacify you, go ahead," he finally agreed, aware that he was growling at her and wishing he wasn't. "Where did you get all these maternal instincts?"

"Julian, I promise you, I don't feel at all maternal toward you." She sank down beside him as he stretched out on his stomach, his face turned away from her. Without further comment she went to work on his bare thigh, starting from the knee and working up toward the puckered scar.

So good, Julian thought, slowly beginning to relax. Her hands felt wonderful. She seemed to know exactly where to knead the muscles. This was what he had been craving all evening. "Just how much hands-on instruction in this kind of thing did you get from that football physical therapist?"

He sensed the smile in her voice. "Actually, the lessons stopped at the neck and shoulders. I'm improvising."

He submitted to the "improvising" with what he hoped seemed like disdainful reluctance, as if he were, indeed, just humoring her. But privately Julian admitted to himself that he had been longing for her touch. He tried to figure out a way to thank her without admitting just how much he'd needed the soothing massage. Perhaps he'd just say thanks very casually when she was done. Or perhaps he'd reach around, take her by the nape of the neck and pull her down onto the bed. He could make love to her to show her how grateful he was.

But would she understand that he was trying to convey gratitude and pleasure? She'd probably accuse him of trying to control her again.

"Julian?"

"Hmmm?" His voice sounded too satisfied and lazy, even to his own ears.

"What made the fire flame in all those colors this afternoon?"

He had to stop and think about what she meant. "Oh, yeah. The colors. You can make any fire do that with a certain powdered chemical that you sprinkle on the flames."

"But when and how?"

"Sara did it just as she cried out and collapsed."

"Oh."

There was a pause while Anne digested that. She seemed to be about to say something else but Julian felt her hesitate then change her mind. Vaguely he wondered what it was she had started to tell him. He wished she didn't feel she had to pick and choose her words.

But his leg was feeling almost magically better now, and the soothing quality of Anne's touch seemed to be the most important thing in the world at the moment. What was she thinking, he wondered. Then he recalled the way he had felt the night he had cuddled and gentled her after the nightmare.

Perhaps, just perhaps, she felt the way he had then; filled with a longing to offer comfort. If that was the case, if he knew for certain that she hadn't lost any respect for him because of his illness and his weak-

ness, then perhaps he could risk letting her know that
he wanted and needed her touch tonight, that he
wasn't merely suffering through the attention.

Julian tried to think of all the ways he could test the
waters before taking the plunge. He was seriously
thinking of starting out with just a straightforward
thank-you when all of a sudden the massage came to
a halt.

"Good night, Julian. I'll see you in the morning."
Anne pulled the wool blankets up around his shoulders and, after hesitating a few seconds while she apparently debated about whether or not to give in to
the impulse to drop a kiss on his cheek, she quietly
turned out the light and left the room.

Lying very still in the darkness, Julian gathered one
hand into a fist and considered the many facets of
frustration.

Anne slowly closed the connecting door and stood
silently for a moment in the solitude of her own room.
Oh, Julian, she thought unhappily, *can't you even tell
me when you're hurting?*

No. He couldn't. Not yet, at any rate. Not willingly.
And he certainly couldn't tell her that he was grateful
for her care. The pride of a strong man was a difficult
thing to handle, she thought wryly. And she very
much doubted that she was the first woman in history
to learn that salient little fact!

Taking a firm grip on her too-vulnerable emotions,
Anne finished readying herself for bed, turned out the
light and ducked under the bed veil. The day had been
instructive in several ways, she admitted ruefully.

Number one, she had learned very quickly that she
was not about to risk Julian's wrath when it came
to dealing with Dan Hargraves. He was right, she
thought. She'd asked for Julian's help, agreed to abide
by his decisions since he was the expert in coping
with nasty people, and it made sense that she should

obey his orders now that the action had begun. But she was not in a mood to forgive him easily for the manner in which he'd chosen to enforce his commands. Nevertheless, she had found herself being very cautious around Dan today. Just as Julian wished.

Well, there was nothing she could do about that little matter. But it had taught her something about herself. On a very fundamental level she had submitted to Julian Aries. The realization was not particularly pleasant.

In an entirely unrelated matter she had found out that she was surprisingly susceptible to suggestion. It still astonished her that she had allowed herself to drift so easily into that strange, half-dazed state this afternoon. She would have to watch herself around the Craven crowd. All this talk of ghosts and legends was obviously getting to her.

Live and learn, Anne told herself, and promptly fell asleep.

IT WAS THE COLD that awakened her a long time later. The same mind-chilling, thick cold that she had felt during Sara's séance that afternoon. She was beginning to recognize it, Anne thought distractedly, as she stirred and groped for the comforter. It was a product of her overactive imagination and she must deal with it as such.

But this time there was something more accompanying the chill. There was a sense of urgency and anger and a distinct feeling that something was very wrong.

Anne opened her eyes and saw the black-haired, dark-eyed woman in riding clothes. This time she stood near the connecting door, and the sensation of stark urgency was a palpable force in the room.

Anne stared, not aware of the fear she had felt the first time the ghost had appeared in her dreams. Perhaps the natural fright was buried beneath the other emotion beating at her. The pale phantom said nothing, but there was no need for verbal communication. Anne got the message quite clearly that something was wrong and that the wrongness was endangering the man she loved.

Without even stopping to remind herself that the vision had to be a part of a dream, Anne pushed back the comforter and slid off the edge of the round bed. Her bare feet felt the cold almost immediately but it was a normal, natural cold, not the dank foggy chill that she felt on some other level.

"Carlota?" she whispered.

The woman in riding clothes shimmered and vanished but Anne knew she would not be able to rest until she had checked Julian's room. The sense of urgency had not disappeared with the specter.

Soundlessly Anne turned the knob on the connecting door and peered into Julian's room. The darkness she had left when she had turned out his lamp was pierced now with a shaft of light from his other door, the one that opened onto the hallway.

And silhouetted in that angle of brightness was Julian. He was standing in his jeans, his hand braced casually against the door as he greeted Sara.

"I am here because I must be here," Sara said with the deceptive simplicity of a Zen master. "I had no choice. The compulsion is strong. Too strong to resist. There is a natural kinship between you and me. I sensed it from the moment I entered this house. There is an essential oneness that must be completed. I have come here tonight to offer that completion."

"Is this all part of the de-ghosting rituals?" Julian asked with bland interest.

Sara shook her head very gently, just enough so that the heavy blond curtain rippled enticingly around her shoulders. "This is only between you and me. You are alone tonight, aren't you, Julian Aries? I saw you enter this room by yourself. The woman you say is your fiancée does not share your bed. I am also alone. I have been most of my life. Do you know what it is like to be a sensitive in a world of blind fools who will not accept what I can see? I exhaust myself in the effort to communicate with those on the other side, just as I did this afternoon, and most of the people watching see it all as just a parlor game. An amusing little trick."

"And it's not?"

"It's no game, Julian. Believe me, at times I wish it were. At times I wish I were just an ordinary woman with an ordinary occupation. But there are so few sensitives to make the necessary contacts. So many presences to be freed. I could never justify abandoning my calling. I would still hear the agony and the pleas of those I should be aiding."

"Sounds like you're trapped in the business, all right."

"We are all trapped in some aspect of life, are we not? Recognizing the trap is not something everyone can do. But I can, and I believe you are a man who also knows the traps of life." Sara reached up to touch his face. "We have so few opportunities of escaping even for a short time. It would be a shame not to take advantage of each chance. Tonight you and I have such a chance, Julian Aries." She smiled wistfully. "Aries. The sign of the zodiac that promises much force and energy. Boldness and strength of will. A man born under that sign can be a dangerous opponent or—" she framed his face between her fingers "—or a demanding lover."

Anne watched the blonde rise on her toes, clearly about to kiss Julian, and decided the whole scene had gone far enough. She pushed open the connecting door and stepped into Julian's room.

"Then again, what's in a name?" she asked brightly, pleased with the way Sara jumped and dropped her hands from Julian's face. "Aries just happens to be Julian's last name, not the sign under which he was born. Sorry about the slight miscalculation, Sara. Because of such minor errors whole evenings can be ruined." She padded forward to stand beside Julian, aware that he was watching her with a gleam of amusement in his eyes. "Run along, dear, and don't fret about that business of an essential oneness with Julian. I'm sure you'll both survive without it. Why don't you go have a chat with Carlota? She needs attention more than Julian does. As you can see, Julian really doesn't need to accept your generous offer. He's not alone, after all."

For an instant the wistful, haunted expression in Sara's eyes disappeared to be replaced by the flashing anger of a woman whose plans have been foiled. Anne took an unholy satisfaction in having been the cause of sweet Sara's ruined bedtime scheme. The other woman stared at her for a long moment, turned on her heel and walked briskly back down the corridor to her own room.

"I gave her the bedroom done in the style of a thirties' musical. You know, the one with the black-and-white steps leading up to the black-and-white bed. Lots of superficial glitz and glitter. A bit theatrical, but I thought it fit her nicely even though she does parade around like a refugee from the flower-child generation." Anne turned away as Julian reached out to firmly close his door but she knew she wasn't going to make it safely back to her own bedroom unscathed. Still, she made a valiant effort, her cold bare feet moving quickly across the hardwood floor.

"Not quite so fast, lady," Julian said behind her. A second later his hand closed solidly over her shoulder. She sighed as he spun her around to face him. "Mind telling me what that little scene was all about?"

"Scene? I didn't cause a scene. Sweet Sara what's-her-name was the one who caused the scene."

"Uh-huh. I know what sweet Sara was doing here. What interests me is what brought you to the rescue."

Anne met his gaze. "You wouldn't believe me if I told you. Frankly, I'm not sure I believe it myself."

Some of the wry humor left Julian's face. "What's that supposed to mean?"

"Well, what actually woke me was the same thing that roused me the other night. A dream about Carlota's ghost. Only it was so incredibly real, Julian. It's hard to describe. It was as if she was trying to tell me something and that it had to do with you. I felt the strongest compulsion to check up on you. I had to make sure you were all right."

"Did you now?" He stroked back a tendril of autumn-colored hair, his face softening in the shadowy light. "You know what I think happened?"

"What?"

"I think that you heard Sara's knock in your sleep and your subconscious translated that into a warning."

"You think I'd have heard her knocking on your door?"

"It's possible. It's just a few feet down the hall from yours, after all."

Anne frowned. "Perhaps." She remembered the shrouding cold that had accompanied the warning sensation. And then she recalled her own suspected weakness when it came to suggestion.

"In any event, you came racing to my rescue," he mused. "Were you jealous, Anne?"

"That little blond con artist has had her eye on you all day," Anne said with a sniff, trying and failing to move out from under Julian's hand.

"Probably because Hargraves was having so little luck with you," Julian murmured. "It was a two-pronged effort right from the start. When you made it clear you weren't going to be an easy target for Dan, Sara decided it was time to test the waters with me. Divide and conquer, remember?"

"You didn't look as though you were trying to fight her off."

"I was curious."

"I'll bet."

Julian shook his head, his amusement growing. "No, seriously. I wanted to hear the pitch."

"You can hear a similar one on any street corner!"

"Well, I sure as hell wasn't hearing it from you."

Anne went pale under the almost casual cruelty. Standing unnaturally still under the restraint of his hand, she lowered her lashes. "No, you weren't, were you?"

Julian groaned and pulled her close, his fingers cupping the back of her head. "Damn, I didn't mean it like that, Anne. Sometimes I say things to you that I wish I hadn't. I don't know what it is about you, honey. I can handle myself so easily around most people. But with you I...never mind." He used his thumbs to lift her chin and his eyes moved searchingly over her face. "Were you really jealous, Anne?"

"In a way," she admitted starkly. "Were you jealous of Dan?"

He hesitated. "In a way." There was another pause and then Julian ventured very cautiously. "But it wasn't that I really believed you'd jump into bed with Hargraves."

Anne summoned a misty smile. "And I wasn't really afraid you'd take Sara up on her offer. I was just thoroughly annoyed that she was making it and that you were listening to it."

"I guess that's how I felt about Hargraves." His

fingers moved lightly down to the soft line of her nape. "Except that I was more than annoyed. I was scared he'd con you into thinking he was an all-right guy. And I was furious that he had the nerve to make a pass. And I was mad at you for even listening to him."

"But you didn't actually think I'd let it go any further," Anne concluded softly.

"No."

"And I didn't really believe you'd invite sweet Sara into your bed."

They stared intently at each other for a long moment, then Anne said quietly, "It's called trust."

Julian's restless hands suddenly clenched around the curve of her shoulders. "Do you trust me, Anne?"

"I've always trusted you. Even when I thought I hated you. You've never lied to me." *Except when you told me you would come back for me. And I understand now why you didn't,* she added silently.

"I'll never give you cause to lose that trust," he whispered huskily. "I swear it."

Anne gathered her courage. "I want the same thing in return. Your trust."

"Yes."

It was the starkness of that single affirmative that told Anne just how rarely he gave the precious commodity. In a flash of perception she realized that Julian Aries had probably seldom trusted anyone or anything in his life. An aching sweetness flowed through her as she comprehended just how much he had given when he said he trusted her.

"Oh, Julian, I'll never betray you," she whispered brokenly, brushing her lips across his mouth. It was a vow and he accepted it as such, holding her fiercely to him so that she was crushed against the hardness of his chest. Her hair flowed over his arm and the hem of the flannel gown wrapped itself around his legs.

The silent bonding held them both in a strange thrall. Anne took hope and courage from it, telling herself that with both physical attraction and trust between them she had the beginnings of a solid foundation on which to build. Julian's love might be a long time coming and it might be an even longer time before he was capable of acknowledging his need of her on some level other than the physical, but she would be patient. Even if it took a lifetime. And in the meantime they would trust each other. A lot of people never got that far, she assured herself. She was lucky.

"Your nightmare," Julian murmured into her hair. "Did it frighten you tonight?"

"No," she replied absently. "It was strange but there wasn't that startled sense of panic I had last time."

"Oh." He went silent again. He seemed vaguely disappointed in something. Then he went on more practically. "Just the same, I'll double-check your doors and windows before you go back to bed. You'll sleep better that way."

She sensed a question hidden in the statement but ignored it as another thought struck her. Anne raised her head away from his shoulder. "You never told me how the security measures looked in this house. You said you were going to make a survey of them."

He nodded. "Pretty dismal. Considering the amount of valuables housed here, I'm surprised Miss Creswell's sister didn't take more precautions. Those vases in the library look like they're worth a lot all by themselves. Not to mention the paintings and that fancy china."

"They're all worth a fortune. That's why Michael thought this would be such a tantalizing piece of bait for Craven and his friends. I have no idea why Miss Creswell's sister didn't install more efficient security measures. I guess she just never felt the need to bother. Probably never had any trouble."

"Times are changing. When this is all over someone should advise the new owner on what to do to protect her property," Julian said thoughtfully. "I wonder if she'd be interested in hiring me?"

Anne held her breath. It was the first time Julian had mentioned a future of any kind. "Are you a real expert on that sort of thing? Locks and bolts and stuff?"

His mouth curved wryly. "And electronic devices. Yeah, I guess you could say I'm an expert. One of the few skills I picked up during my, uh, former career. I just never thought of it as particularly marketable."

"Are you kidding? People pay a lot these days for security advice. Industry has a great need for it as well as private individuals such as Miss Creswell. She'd hire you in a minute to redo this place," Anne declared strongly.

"You think so?"

"Definitely."

"Hmmm. Well, it's something to think about. My career options have seemed rather limited for the past six months," he growled. Then his eyes narrowed. "Are you sure that nightmare didn't bother you this time?"

"Worried I might yet have hysterics?"

"No, it's just that last time you were kind of upset."

Suddenly something clicked in Anne's brain and she stifled a small smile. "Yes, I was, wasn't I? Perhaps the only reason I didn't go bananas this time was because I was busy defending your virtue."

Julian didn't seem to see any humor in the situation. He appeared to be searching for words. "Now that you've saved me from a fate worse than death, I wonder if you'll have any trouble, uh, getting back to sleep. When you're lying all alone there in that silly bed you're liable to start remembering how real the nightmare was."

"It certainly did seem real."

"Maybe it would help you get to sleep faster if I rubbed your back for a while," Julian offered with seeming casualness.

It was no slick, double-edged offer, Anne realized. Julian really did want to rub her back. He was, in a very tentative, uncertain manner, trying to provide her with some of the comfort she had given him earlier this evening. And even if she didn't need it to help her over the effects of the nightmare, she hungered for it for other reasons.

It was another small step forward, Anne thought as she nodded her agreement to his suggestion and led him toward the connecting door. Julian might not know how to ask for tender loving care, but if he was learning to offer it he was definitely making progress.

"Thank you, Julian," she murmured as she stretched out on her stomach on the round bed. "You have no idea how real Carlota's vision seemed tonight. And the room felt so cold. It was very odd. Do you know that I thought I half felt her presence in the living room this afternoon when Sara went into her trance bit?"

Julian sat down beside her, his powerful hands moving over her shoulders with a strong, kneading action that was unexpectedly relaxing. "I think this whole scene is really getting to you," he declared seriously. "If we weren't so enmeshed in it and hadn't already exposed Miss Creswell's house to Craven, I'd seriously consider calling it all off."

"It's too late for that. Besides, it should be all over soon. Sara will treat us to one or two more séances during which we'll hear the so-called truth about Carlota. Then she'll pronounce the poor woman 'freed' and away will go Craven and crowd. Phase one will be over. What happens next, Julian? Will you keep an eye on this place personally or hire someone else to do it?"

"Twenty-four-hour surveillance jobs are impossible to conduct alone. I'll bring in some outside help."

"Who?"

"I have some contacts," he said slowly. "Some people who could use the work."

"Other folks from your particular unemployment line?" Anne questioned dryly.

"I guess you could say that. My former line of work tends to have a few occupational hazards. A lot of people wind up taking early retirement," Julian muttered.

Anne hated the note of roughness that had entered his voice. His fingers seemed to be tensing on her shoulders. "Julian?"

"Yes?"

"Is Aries more than your last name? Is it also the sign under which you were born?"

His hands went still on the curve of her shoulders. "You mean you're not sure? Even after that little squelching speech to Sara?"

"I don't even know when your birthday is. All I know is that you had one during the past year. But I somehow think you might be an Aries."

"Why?"

She turned over lazily, her smile warm and welcoming in the darkness as her love thrummed through her veins. "Well, I suspect Sara was right about you making a dangerous opponent."

Gleaming desire began to replace the honest concern that had been reflected in his catlike eyes. "You think so?"

Anne nodded, feeling strangely shy as she found herself initiating the lovemaking. But if Julian could show her some TLC, she could show him a little tender love. He hadn't had much of it in his life and she had so much to give him.

"Yes, I think so. And I do know she was right about

the other. You are a very demanding lover." Anne reached up to pull him down to her and heard the husky growl of unadulterated masculine pleasure that rumbled in his chest.

He came to her with barely restrained power, parting her legs with his hands to make a place for himself at her hearth. His weight bore her deeply into the sheets, cutting off the rest of the outside world completely. She knew the roughness of his chest hair against her flowering nipples, delighted in the impact of his hips as she raised her lower body to meet him.

Then, when she thought he was about to plunge into her she found herself being deliciously tormented by the feel of him at the threshold of her aching desire. Deliberately he teased and tantalized, thrusting into her only fractionally and then withdrawing almost at once. Again and again he repeated the wildly sensuous torture until Anne's fingers were clenched into the skin of his shoulders and her legs were a vise around his waist. Helplessly, demandingly, pleadingly she begged him to take her completely.

And when he did, Anne cried out his name in a litany of unraveling excitement.

Lost in the overwhelming assault on her senses, Anne didn't realize until much later that she still didn't know whether or not Julian was really an Aries.

The fierce, throbbing purr of the huge cat who had captured her was the only answer she sought to hear that night.

9

ANNE DID NOT SLEEP WELL that night and it surprised her. Considering the passionate demands Julian had made on her she should have been pleasantly exhausted.

His lovemaking had been different this time. She wasn't quite certain how to define the difference but it seemed to Anne that there was less of a sense of desperation in it. It was as if Julian had been trying very hard to accept the gift she was trying to give. He had seemed enthralled with her gentle boldness, fascinated with her willingness to initiate the lovemaking. And he had also seemed determined not to question his luck, Anne decided with a flash of perceptive humor. He had been tired earlier, and she knew the couple of hours' sleep he'd had before sweet Sara came knocking on his door probably hadn't been nearly enough to revitalize him. But Anne would never have known that, by the way he urged her on with husky words of excitement and need.

In all honesty, Anne thought, Julian wasn't the only one who had been rather astonished by her soft aggression. She herself had been more than a little surprised. She had intended to sleep alone that night. But the scene in Julian's room had changed all her intentions.

So why couldn't she sleep, she wondered, turning restlessly on her side. Julian was solidly out beside her, sprawled over a good portion of the round bed. His head was turned away from her, and the comforter had slipped down around his sleek shoulders.

In the pale light of a watery moon she could see the scar that slashed across his back.

Anne wondered if he would ever tell her the full story of what had happened on that last mission. There was no point pushing for it. He had drawn some very fierce lines over which she dared not cross. Perhaps he would never be able to talk about it. What was it he had said? The best thing to do with a nightmare was to put it behind you.

A few days ago she was convinced she had been wrong to intrude on Julian's self-imposed privacy. Now she didn't know what to think. At times such as tonight, it seemed he was making progress. There had been talk of the future and talk of trust.

At other times Anne felt that she had no right to interfere with whatever form of healing Julian had chosen for himself. The risk wasn't just to him, she acknowledged bleakly, it was to her, as well. She was making herself far too vulnerable, leaving herself open to pain. Julian might be changing a little but his bitterness and pride still lay close to the surface. He was still capable of turning on the one who loved him and slashing her with a carelessly cruel swipe of his claws. She must not forget that.

But even that knowledge, as uneasy as it made her, did not account for the feeling of restlessness tonight. She lay staring over Julian's bare shoulders at the weak moon on the ocean. Some of the fog had cleared, she realized idly. But it would probably be back by morning.

Some of the fog had cleared. She found herself repeating the observation. Cleared enough so that, with care, a person could make her way down to the beach. It would be tricky, of course. The cliff face was treacherous even in daylight. But with caution and a flashlight it would be possible. . . .

Good grief! Anne shut her eyes in momentary

disbelief. It was utterly incomprehensible that she should even be considering such a thing. Was she out of her mind, she wondered. What idiot would think of going down to the beach in the middle of the night?

Carlota.

Anne drew a deep, steadying breath. Carlota had gone down to the beach on a night such as this. A night in late fall when the fog had been uncertain, offering both peril and concealment.

Uneasily Anne glanced around the darkened room, vastly relieved not to see any lingering shades of her dream ghost. She was getting fanciful. The night and the mystery of the house were getting to her. That was all there was to it. Julian had warned her obliquely that it could become difficult to tell the difference between reality and illusion.

Anne sighed and tried to make herself relax. But the vague restlessness didn't go away and she was still half awake when the pale glow of another fog-bound day finally arrived.

Julian opened his eyes to find Anne lying quietly awake beside him. He watched her in silence for a moment, aware that her attention was on the dismal weather scene outside the window. He was feeling better than he had in months, he realized with a sense of satisfaction. Well rested, no bad aches or pains and he was even feeling hungry. It had been ages since he'd had a genuine appetite for breakfast.

Breakfast wasn't the only thing for which he felt an appetite. With lazy anticipation he put out a hand to stroke the contour of Anne's throat. She looked so soft and tousled this morning. Memories of the way she had pulled him down to her last night flickered through his head.

But the moment his fingers touched her skin she stirred and turned too quickly. There was a tension in her he didn't understand. She had moved as if his touch had startled her.

"Anne?" He murmured her name, leaning closer to drop a possessive kiss on her mouth. "Everything okay? How did you sleep?" He smiled in anticipation of the appropriate answer.

"Fine."

Julian blinked, lazily aware that the small word was a lie and wondering why she would bother with such a tiny falsehood. "Sure?"

"What time is it? It feels rather late." She twisted around to find the clock.

"It's not late. Prue won't even be arriving for another hour or so. Relax. We've got lots of time." Julian traced a teasing fingertip down to the opening of the flannel nightgown. Deliberately he pinned her gaze as he probed beneath the fabric. "Hungry?"

"No."

Julian hid his disappointment. Perhaps she hadn't understood the double entendre. "Not even for this?" He let his fingers glide warmly over her breast, delighting in the womanly fullness of her.

"Julian I ... I'm not ... that is, I don't ...."

He could feel the way her nipple was beginning to harden under his touch. Surely she wasn't going to lie there and tell him she didn't want him! But something was wrong this morning. The tension in her was not that of physical desire but it was very real.

"Are you regretting last night?" he demanded gruffly, unaware of the way his palm suddenly weighed more heavily on her breast, as though he would trap her.

"Julian, I think ... I think we may be rushing things." A vivid intensity swirled in her blue-green eyes.

"It's a little late to worry about that now, isn't it?" he tried coolly.

"I don't know whether it's too late or not. I only

know I had no right to track you down in Colorado. You should have been allowed all the time you wanted to be by yourself. You should have the right to take your time...."

"Anne, we are discussing the possibilities of a little early morning loving, not my past or my future," he told her, aware of a vague irritation seeping into his voice. What was the matter with her? She had initiated matters last night. She had no right to change her mind this morning, he decided with a measure of masculine indignation. He was half tempted to demonstrate quite forcefully that he wasn't going to allow her to play the tease. He might not be quite the same man he had been when he'd left her six months ago but that didn't mean he was so weak she could now manipulate him.

"I'm sorry, Julian. It's just that I feel a little odd this morning. A bit nervous or something. I'll be glad when this is all over."

He didn't like the absolute certainty with which she made that declaration. It sounded very much as though she wanted to be rid of him. "Do you think," he growled in soft warning, "that I'm going to let you walk back out of my life after this business with Craven is finished?"

She seemed to gather herself. "I think we both need time, Julian."

Anger simmered now in place of the lazy morning passion that had been building in him. He knew it probably was reflected in his eyes because he saw the wariness that came into her own gaze. "I'm willing to give you time, lady, but I'm not going to let you blow hot and cold. You're not going to seduce me one night and then pull away in the morning. I never would have guessed you were the kind of female who uses sex to tease and confuse a man. But if you are, you'd better realize right away that I'm not the kind of male to let you play that game."

"Oh, Julian, I never meant to play games with you," she protested.

"Then why the coy act this morning?"

"I'm not being coy! I told you, I just feel a little restless. A little uneasy. I'm not at all sure we're developing this relationship in the proper way. In fact, I'm fairly certain I've handled matters all wrong."

"Like I said, it's too late to change your mind." But he was confounded by her very genuine agitation. She *was* nervous and tense, and he wasn't at all sure of how to deal with her. The last thing he wanted to do was drive her away, he thought. "Look, Anne. I'm not some kind of monster. Before you arrived at my door in Colorado I'd been six months without a woman...."

Instantly he realized he'd said something horribly wrong. He had been attempting to explain that wanting her first thing in the morning after having made love to her during the night was hardly abnormal. But she reacted as if he'd slapped her.

"Is that all you've been doing for the past couple of nights? Making up for six months of abstinence?" she hissed, scrambling off the edge of the bed.

"Anne, for crying out loud! You know that's not what I meant! What's the matter with you this morning? Last night...."

But she wasn't sticking around to hear his analysis of last night. The door to the red-and-brass bathroom slammed firmly behind her incensed figure. Julian threw himself back down on the pillows with a groan and cursed himself for being an idiot. When he was finished with that project he went to work on the female of the species, finding terms even less complimentary.

Julian had vacated her bedroom by the time Anne finished her morning shower. She opened the bathroom door cautiously, peering around at the bed before entering. There was a sense of both relief and disappointment in finding she had the sheikh's room to herself.

Hastily she dressed in a pair of olive-drab trousers and a matching designer version of a military style shirt. Together with the wide leather belt and the short cuffed boots, the effect was rakishly chic and it gave Anne a certain degree of inner fortitude. She needed it today she realized later as she headed downstairs alone. The strange restlessness was still invading her blood and she felt taut with a vague tension.

A walk on the beach after breakfast might be nice, she thought, as she entered the breakfast room and found Prue pouring herself a cup of coffee.

"Good morning, Anne. How did you sleep?"

"Fine." There was certainly no point going into uninteresting details of a restless night. "That coffee looks good."

"Ummm." Prue sipped enthusiastically on her cup. "I had some before I left the house, but after driving through that fog, I needed another cup. It's like the inside of a can of gray paint out there."

"You shouldn't have taken the risk," Anne admonished with a frown. "I could certainly handle the cooking for this bunch for a couple of days."

"Well, if it's this bad again tomorrow morning, I might take you up on the offer. We get stretches of fog like this along the coast a few times during the year, and the car accident rate always skyrockets because of it."

"That settles it. Assuming it's safe enough to drive home this evening, don't you dare attempt coming to work tomorrow until it clears off."

"Thanks." Prue smiled. "My husband was a little upset. I told him you needed me because of all these ghost hunters to feed and tidy up after." Prue took another sip of her coffee. "A bit of a disappointment, isn't it?"

"What's that?" Anne was thinking again of a walk on the beach.

"This ghost hunting business. I mean that séance yesterday was rather bland. I expected a lot more excitement."

"I know," Anne said thoughtfully. "So did I." And she realized that was the truth. According to her brother's notes the Craven crowd usually put on a fairly exciting show. So far all the Creswell ghost had received was a somewhat half-hearted attempt at contact. She had expected that real phonies, such as Craven and his bunch were supposed to be, would resort to more theatrical effects. On the other hand, perhaps the calm approach convinced people they were genuine in their efforts. Then her mind returned to the beach.

Would it be possible to navigate the path down to the cove in this fog? Last night it would have been easier. At least then she would have had the pale moonlight. This morning she wouldn't be able to see more than a few feet in front of her.

Ridiculous. The very notion of going for a walk in this gray soup was idiotic. Anne shook off the idea as Sara walked into the room followed by Dan Hargraves. Both greeted Prue and Anne politely, Sara acting as if nothing at all had happened the previous night, and made casual comments on the weather.

"Does this kind of gloomy weather help in making contact with the ghosts?" Prue asked interestedly as she carted in a tray of toast and bacon.

"Surprisingly enough it does," Dan said easily, helping himself to the toast. "Atmospheric effects sometimes do seem to release more energy that a presence can, in turn, utilize for contact. That's probably why most of the old legends involve dark and stormy nights," he concluded with a grin.

"Perhaps it is that the sensitives are able to tune in more easily when the weather is unsettled," Sara offered vaguely. "Where is Thomas?"

"I saw him in the library with Julian," Dan said. "They looked pretty involved in a discussion. I didn't want to interrupt."

"A most interesting discussion," Craven said genially as he strode into the room followed by a quiet-faced Julian. "Mr. Aries was just telling me that Miss Creswell has plans to modernize the rather antiquated security measures in this old place. I certainly would, if it belonged to me. There are some extremely valuable items here."

If a silent message was passed among the three ghost hunters, Anne certainly couldn't detect it. Part of the scheme had been to put the pressure on them to make their move sooner than usual by implying that security was soon going to be tightened.

"When is she going to have the work done?" Sara asked idly.

"In a couple of weeks," Julian said as if rather uninterested. "Or so she said. Wasn't that the date she said the security expert would arrive and begin installing the electronics, Anne?"

"Yes, I think so," Anne managed politely. And wondered privately if this whole plan had even a prayer of working. Perhaps Michael had been wrong about Craven and crowd. Perhaps they were merely honest psychic investigators after all.

"When's the next séance going to take place?" Prue asked.

Craven smiled and nodded at Sara. "It's up to her. How do the vibrations feel, Sara?"

"Weak but present. I think it's worth a try today."

"This morning?" Dan prodded.

"Yes, that will be fine," Sara agreed softly.

The second séance took place after breakfast and was set up in much the same manner as the first. Sara asked that a fire be built and Julian complied. Once again the small group sat in the living room of the fog-shrouded house and watched Sara chant herself into a trance.

But this time Anne felt no odd sense of disorientation. Rather the urge to take the walk on the beach seemed to be pushing out all other interests. Julian, more silent than usual, took his place beside her. He seemed aware of her restlessness and it appeared to annoy him. Several times Anne felt his brooding glance on her profile. Impatiently she ignored it and tried to concentrate on Sara's little show.

"Carlota, we have come to hear the truth. Tell us your story so that you can be free. We will believe," Sara intoned in her soft singsong.

Over and over again, eyes closed, seated in front of the fire in her lotus position, Sara called for the phantom lady. Anne felt her own impatience grow steadily. This was ridiculous. Carlota wasn't in this room. A walk on the beach would be far more revealing than listening to Sara's chanting act. She was seriously wondering if she could slip away from the group when Sara's body went suddenly taut.

"Yes," the other woman breathed almost soundlessly. "We are here. I can feel you, Carlota. Tell us...."

Silence descended on the group of people in front of the fire as Sara waited in a tense, listening pose. Dan was busy taping the session and Craven sat forward, his hands steepled, his face a study in concentration. Prue was hunched in a posture of breathless anticipation. And Julian looked laconically bored.

Anne stared out the window, wondering how fog-bound the path down to the beach would be right now. If she were to slip away she could be down in the cove before anyone knew she had left.

No, Julian would be well aware of her leaving the room. Annoyed at that fact, Anne continued to sit dutifully while Sara exchanged messages with Carlota's nonexistent ghost.

"We understand, Carlota. I will tell the others. They will believe."

Tension hummed in the atmosphere and Anne had to give Sara credit for creating it with her intense attitude and apparent belief in what she saw. Prue didn't look disappointed in today's séance, even if there were no visible manifestations.

And then, quite suddenly, it was all over. Sara sobbed heavily, taking great gasps of air, and then she collapsed attractively. Dan reached out to catch her. Once again brandy was brought, and Sara smiled apologetically as she sipped.

"A simple enough story," she explained as Prue asked for all the details. "Carlota says that she was not running away with her lover the night that her husband discovered and killed her. She says she and Diego, that's the lover's name, had agreed that their love could not be fulfilled without bringing dishonor on both households. She says she met with Diego one last time to say farewell and that her husband descended on them. He wouldn't listen to reason. She shouted for Diego to leave, saying she would explain it all to her husband. Diego fled but Carlota was unable to talk sense into the enraged man who thought he had discovered her in a thoroughly compromising position."

"So her husband strangled her instead of listening to the truth, hmmm?" Prue nodded in satisfaction.

"The poor woman died violently and under a curtain of dishonor. In those days outward appearances meant everything. She died knowing that the world would think her a faithless wife. The last conscious thought she had was one of wishing for justice." Sara sighed in commiseration. "She wanted the world to know the truth—that, in spite of temptation, she had been faithful."

"That fierce, dying desire for justice combined with the violence of her passing must have been the factors that kept her bound to this house," Craven observed. "What now? Do you think she's been freed?"

"Thomas, I'm too exhausted to be able to sense her presence, even if she's still here. By tomorrow morning I will know. Every night I've been here I've been very much aware of her presence. If she's still trapped here, I'll sense her again during the night. If she's free, I'll know she's gone."

Craven nodded. "And if she is, then we can take our leave in the morning. Wouldn't want to charge Miss Creswell for any extra unnecessary time, would we?" He patted Sara gently. "Got all your notes, Dan?"

"I've got the session down on tape, but, as usual, I'll want to talk to Sara in detail before she has a chance to forget any pertinent information. How about it, Sara? Feel up to our usual analysis?"

"Yes, I think so," the blonde nodded, sitting up on the sofa where Dan had placed her after she collapsed. She set aside the brandy and smiled wearily. "It's fading fast, Dan. You'd better hurry up with your questions."

Dan glanced around at the others. "Mind if we do this part in private? It's difficult for Sara to reconstruct everything when she has an audience."

"Of course not," Anne said quickly, leading the way out of the living room. "Take your time."

The others followed her out but Anne didn't stop to discuss the events. She headed straight upstairs to her bedroom, closing the door firmly behind her. Then she went to the closet and dug out her red jacket. She had to get out of the house before this restlessness drove her nuts.

When she emerged from her room several minutes later she could hear the voices of Julian and Craven in the hall below the stairs. On an impulse, because she didn't want to bother with a lot of questions and explanations, Anne headed for the back stairs. They led down to the kitchen. Anne descended in silence and then let herself out into the thick, gray mist.

She had to take her time, but the going wasn't quite as treacherous as she had imagined. It was possible to see several feet ahead, and that was enough to be sure of her footing. The sound of the surf in the cove below the cliffs guided her in the right direction.

Cautiously, slipping a bit now and then on the damp rocky path, Anne made her way down the short cliff to the sea. She had taken a walk on the beach only once during her stay, and on that occasion had headed south from the cove. Today she would head north. She was quite certain of her direction.

Pebbles churned underfoot as she neared the bottom and Anne nearly lost her balance. She landed on her feet amid a shower of rocky debris a few minutes later.

The first thing she realized was that the tide was out. Getting around the jutting northern tip of the rock wall that formed the cove would be no problem this morning. Having always lived in the Midwest she knew little about the rhythm of the tides, but it occurred to her that there were probably times when the entire floor of the cove was under water. Little pools among the rocks testified to the repeated return of the sea.

The foggy mist swirled around her as she made her way toward the northern tip of the cove. For some reason the urge to explore that region was irresistible today. Doing so would pacify the restlessness that seemed to be flooding her bloodstream.

"Anne!"

She stopped suddenly as Julian's voice came at her through the fog.

"Anne, where are you?"

Irritation mingled with a reluctant realization that she would have to answer, so Anne halted.

"Julian!" she called back. "I'm just taking a walk. Don't worry about me!"

There was no response but she sensed that he was starting down the cliff face. Suddenly another thought occurred to her, one that made her forget her earlier decision to explore the northern end of the cove.

Julian had no business exposing himself to this dank, damp, chill fog. He should be keeping warm in the house. There was no telling, but the cold air might very well bring on another attack of his strange fever.

"Julian?" Frowning she tried to determine his progress down the cliff by sound. He was moving much more quietly than she had. Another occupational skill he'd probably picked up in his former career, she thought wryly.

"Right here," he growled, startling her by looming out of the fog. He wore an expression of tight-lipped anger. "What on earth do you think you're doing?"

"What am I doing?" she retorted, surveying his worn leather jacket and jeans. "You're the one who should be asked that. I'm merely taking a walk. You have no business at all being outside on a day like this! Don't you have any common sense? Are you deliberately trying to bring on another bout of that fever?"

He came forward, his hands shoved into the pockets of the old jacket. "What kind of idiot takes a walk on a day like this?"

"I felt like it. There's no harm in it for me. You're the one who should know better than to be outside. Go back to the house, Julian, I don't want to have you getting sick again." She turned away, intending to start back toward the far end of the cove but found herself dragged to a jolting stop under Julian's rough fingers.

When he spun her around she realized that he was blazingly angry. Anne caught her breath as his tawny eyes glittered. His hand was clamped tightly around her shoulder. Instinctively she went very still, all thought of continuing her exploration forgotten as she confronted the lion enraged.

"I'm sorry if my being ill is a burden on you," he began savagely.

"Oh, Julian, I never meant—"

"Just keep in mind that I never asked you to deal with that blasted fever. You're the one who showed up on my doorstep in the middle of the night. You're the one who insisted on playing nurse. If you found the whole bit boring, you have no one but yourself to blame."

"Julian, you know perfectly well I never—"

"You wanted my help, you said. My protection. Well, you've got it. But one of the agreements we made is that I'm in charge, remember? You will do as I say. And right now I'm saying I don't want you going for lonely walks in the fog. This is treacherous country. You know nothing of tides and you know nothing of the terrain. Furthermore, since part of my job is to keep an eye on you, the last thing I'm going to do is let you wander off alone."

"I only wanted to take a walk, Julian. I've been feeling a little restless cooped up in that house."

"You've been acting very strange all day," he countered. "Ever since this morning when you flounced off to the bathroom in high dudgeon."

"Well, what did you expect after you implied you were trying to make up for lost time because you hadn't had a woman in six months?" she flared, angered to the point of recklessness.

"You'll have to forgive my animalistic desires along with my tendency to fall sick at inconvenient times. Just keep in mind that sometimes you get what you ask for in this life and you asked for me. You've got me. If I don't live up to your expectations, that's tough. You're stuck with me at the moment. Now get your sweet tail back up that cliff before I drag you up it."

Anne swallowed, knowing when she was definitely going to lose. No point in dragging it out. Julian was quite capable of doing exactly as he threatened. She gave him a bitter, resentful glare and then she stepped pointedly around him, heading for the path up the cliff.

She climbed in silence, aware of him directly beneath her. Several of the wet pebbles loosened by her passage undoubtedly struck him, but Julian said nothing. His anger beat at her as she moved upward, a tangible force that made her edgy and tense. Neither of them spoke until they were on top of the cliff, walking back toward the house. Then Julian said curtly, "About the matter of my, uh, animalistic desires—"

"What about them?"

He took a breath. "You misunderstood me this morning."

"Did I?"

"I never meant to imply that the only reason I wanted to make love to you was because I'd spent the past six months exploring the joys of abstinence!"

"Really?" she drawled flippantly.

"Anne, I wanted to make love to you this morning because... because I wanted you," he exploded tightly. "I've always wanted you. Since the moment I met you, in fact. And you know it."

Anne's hands clenched into fists in the pockets of her red jacket. "Do I?"

"Yes, damn it, you do! Because you've wanted me from the beginning, too."

Anne winced, unable to think of a fast counter to that. It was the truth. "Are you by any chance, in your own inimitable style, trying to apologize for your rather gauche remark in bed this morning?"

"I'm not apologizing, I'm explaining," he snapped.

Anne suddenly grinned, unable to stifle the flash of humor. "Ah, yes, but for you, Julian, I think that constitutes an apology. Probably the only one I'll ever get. I shall savor it."

He eyed her warily. "Does that mean you're going to stop acting so oddly?"

"Have I really been acting that strangely?" she asked curiously.

"You've been, well, distant. As if you had something on your mind. Your temper is short and you haven't seemed particularly interested in the performance of our psychic investigators."

"I told you this morning that I feel tense. Restless. I can't explain it, Julian. I guess this whole thing is getting to me. I'll be glad when it's over."

"Is it this ghost scene that's bothering you or is it us?" he asked bluntly. "You said something this morning about wanting time." Julian's eyes were straight ahead, focused on the huge dark bulk of the house as they approached it through the fog.

Anne sensed the tightness in him and knew he didn't know how to talk about their relationship.

"I think it would be a good idea," she murmured gently. "You have to admit that matters got out of hand this past week."

"Because we went to bed together? Is that what you call getting out of hand?"

"You, I take it, don't see it that way?" she asked dryly.

He shrugged. "No. As long as you and I are around each other, the sex is inevitable."

Anger flashed again in her. Today, in her unusually nervous mood, she seemed to be letting all his casual gibes get to her. "Well, if proximity is the only thing that affects your love life, we can certainly cure that. You can sleep in your own room tonight, Julian!"

10

SEX WASN'T THE ONLY THING that was inevitable, Anne decided much later that night as she crawled alone into bed. If she stayed around Julian Aries she was going to find herself more and more firmly bound to him. But then, perhaps her love for him had been inevitable from the beginning.

Restlessly Anne fluffed her pillow and turned to stare out the window. The fog still clung. But for some reason she was quite sure that, with the aid of a flashlight, she could probably make it down the cliff.

Carlota had found her way down those cliffs one fog-shrouded night. But she hadn't been wearing a black lace gown when she tried it. She'd had on men's-style riding clothes that she had fashioned in secret.

Anne sat up suddenly in bed, startled at how absolutely certain she was of the facts that had just popped into her head. She *knew*, in a way she couldn't explain, that Carlota had gone down to the cove at night. There she had left something...something very important.

Annoyed with herself Anne tried to halt the direction of her thoughts. It wasn't as though she didn't have other matters on which to speculate! Julian, for instance.

Julian, who had said almost nothing to her since dinner. Actually, he'd said very little since he'd force-marched her back up the cliff. But he had appeared in the opening of the communicating door just before going to bed to remind her to lock her hall door.

"Are you worried about something?" she'd asked.

"Craven and his friends are leaving in the morning. I don't want them to get any last-minute ideas," was all he'd said dryly.

He had sealed himself in his own room before she could ask what sort of ideas. His irritation and impatience had been palpable. Anne knew she wasn't behaving with her normal degree of equanimity, but she was powerless to explain her own nervous tension. She lay in bed and wished Julian hadn't caught up with her before she'd had a chance to finish exploring the northern tip of the cove.

There was an answer down there, Anne told herself, staring wide-eyed into the darkness beyond the window. A finish.

The compulsion to go down to the cove became overwhelming. The air seemed to be shimmering between Anne's bed and the window. Tautly she waited for the figure in riding clothes to materialize, but nothing happened.

My God, Anne thought dazedly, *I must be out of my mind to be looking for ghosts.*

But the ghost had come looking for her, something whispered in her head. The answers and the ending lie in the cove. The northern end of the cove.

Anne shook her head, trying to clear it. The urge to go down the cliff only increased to unbearable intensity. Nothing could force her down to the cove, she knew with certainty. But there was a plea behind the compulsion—a plea that caught at her. She wanted to pacify that pleading—bring peace to whatever called. The other woman from a different time had appealed to her because she sensed that Anne understood the undeniable demands of love.

With sudden decision, Anne pushed back the covers and padded over to the closet to find her jeans and a white knit top. Hurriedly she tugged on her boots and found the jacket she had left lying across a chair. Then, very, very softly she unlocked her door and went out into the hall.

The house seemed to be filled with an inner gloom tonight that went beyond normal nighttime shadows. There was no noise and Anne found herself taking care on the staircase.

Just as Carlota had that fateful night.

Once more the unbidden knowledge flowed into Anne's head. Carlota had taken a lantern to the edge of the cliff. But this was the twentieth century, and Anne found a flashlight in a kitchen drawer.

She didn't turn on the light until she was outside, and then it barely cut a swath through the murky darkness. As it had that afternoon, the pounding of the sea served as a guide.

Anne was almost at the cliff's edge searching for the beginning of the pebbly path that led down to the cove when an uneasy prickling sensation made her whirl around.

"Who's there?" she demanded tautly, playing the flashlight across the murk. It came to rest on a curtain of pale hair. "Sara. What in the world...?" And then she saw the ugly gun in Sara's fist. Anne went very still, aware of a surge of fear and adrenaline invading her system. "Sara, I have to tell you, you lose that sweet, flower-child appeal when you're holding a gun."

"Since the appeal didn't work on your lover, there's no point overdoing the act, is there?" Sara remarked, no longer sounding so wistful and gentle as she once had. Instead there was a hard, utterly cold note in her voice.

"Mind telling me why the gun?" Not knowing what else to do, Anne kept the light fixed on the younger woman.

"It's simple enough. Because your name isn't Anne Melton. Your name is Anne Silver."

Anne closed her eyes briefly. "How long have you known?"

"Since the beginning."

"Where's Craven? And Dan?" It was ludicrous, but Anne couldn't think of anything else to ask under the circumstances. It was obvious there was no point denying her identity. Stupid plan. Julian had been right.

"Craven and Dan are taking care of Mr. Aries," Sara assured her. "We all thought I'd be able to handle you by myself. And I think we were all correct, don't you?"

"I get the feeling you're enjoying this."

"I am," Sara acknowledged calmly. "It's rather satisfying to pull the rug out from under you. What did you hope to accomplish, Miss Silver? Did you think we would be so easily tricked? Your brother obviously did. Perhaps stupidity runs in the family."

"You tried to kill him, didn't you?"

"Next time we'll make sure we're successful." Sara smiled. "As successful as we're going to be tonight with you and Aries. What fools you were!"

"How did you know?" Anne knew she was going to have to start thinking clearly, but at this point all she could manage to do was keep the flashlight reasonably level and keep asking questions. What was happening to Julian?

"About you? Oh, it was simple enough. When Miss Creswell hired us and informed us she'd have her niece handle the arrangements we took the single extra step of finding out about the 'niece.' It seems there isn't one. Only a nephew who's stationed in Europe. We wouldn't normally have taken the trouble to check, but lately, what with one thing and another, we've had to be a bit more cautious. I'm sure you can understand."

"And tonight you're planning more accidents?" Anne breathed.

"An unfortunate fall over the cliff. Not here near the path, though. The cliff isn't high enough here to make it look effective. No, I think it will have to be out there at the far end of the cove. Might as well get ready. Move, Anne Silver."

Anne considered her options and found them exceedingly limited. "You don't dare shoot me. If I'm found with a bullet in me it's going to be a little difficult for the authorities to render an 'accidental death' verdict."

"Don't think we haven't planned this very well," Sara said chuckling. "I'll shoot if I must. It will be made to look like a lovers' quarrel in that case. Aries will be made to look as though he pulled the trigger and then committed suicide. Take your choice, the sea or a bullet."

"I might survive the sea," Anne pointed out calmly. Under a prodding motion from Sara's gun she began moving along the top of the cliffs. The water below was not particularly violent tonight. A rather light surf, in fact. And somewhere along here there was the deep pool where the waves surged in and out almost lazily. If one jumped while the waves were on their inward course there would be plenty of deep water to absorb the impact. Farther along, however, a person could easily get dashed against the rocks.

"You'll be unconscious when you go into the sea, I'm afraid," Sara explained kindly. "Both you and Julian. There's not much chance of surviving the ocean if you've been knocked out, is there?"

Anne said nothing, using the flashlight to pick a path along the rocks and occasionally allowing the beam to play over the water. A few more feet should bring her to the section of cliff that formed a backdrop for the deep water pool below. Sara followed from a safe distance but the other woman couldn't stay too far back. She couldn't risk losing Anne in the fog.

The mist roiled and twisted, sometimes parting to reveal a clear path and a stretch of water, at other times closing in so thickly that the beam from Anne's flashlight barely penetrated. Anne noticed that during the moments when the fog swirled most densely, Sara came closer to her quarry. As long as Anne was holding the light, she realized, she was making a target of herself for the blonde's gun.

"How did you know I'd left the house tonight, Sara?"

"We had planned to make our move tonight. I was about to come and get you when you very obligingly opened the door to your room and trotted down the stairs. I merely followed you while Thomas and Dan went to finish the business with your lover. You know, I was rather sorry my little play for Julian didn't work the other night. He's quite interesting in some ways. In spite of the limp and that scar on his face, there's something intriguing about him. Too bad he's unemployed and on your side. I prefer my men rich and devoted to me." Sara laughed.

"Like Thomas Craven?" Anne hazarded, thinking of less-than-paternal pats.

"Yes, Thomas is quite rich now and quite devoted. He doesn't know I made that little side trip to see Julian last night. I'm afraid he wouldn't approve."

"What about Dan?"

"Oh, Dan and I leave each other well enough alone. We're merely business partners. We make a good team. Our partnership has been most lucrative."

"Sara...." Anne hesitated, her curiosity getting the better of her. "Are you at all psychic or is the whole thing an act?"

"All an act. I'm afraid I don't believe in ghosts any more than you do. Too bad you really didn't get the full benefit of one of our performances. We just didn't feel it was worth the trouble to bring on all the bells and whistles. After all, you weren't going to live long enough to appreciate it. Normally we do the whole bit. Even achieve a 'manifestation' of the presence. It's all done with a lot of sophisticated gadgetry we normally carry around. Most of our clients love it."

"I see. Then you saw or felt nothing during that first séance?" Anne asked softly.

"I never see or feel anything strange during a séance, except the gullibility of my audience," Sara murmured. "Slow down. I wouldn't want to lose you now, would I? Blast this fog! I should have brought my own flashlight!"

At that moment the chill wind off the sea parted the mist long enough for Anne to determine that she was in the vicinity of the deep water she sought. Almost immediately the fog closed back in, whirling thickly around her. Anne knew she wasn't going to get a better chance. She also realized in that instant that for a few seconds the flashlight she held was the only point of visual reference Sara could possibly have until the momentary coil of fog lifted.

Anne hurled the flashlight from her, heedless of the direction, and threw herself down onto her stomach.

"Damn you!" Sara screamed in frustrated fury. A second later the gun in her hand roared. Before the sound had even faded into the night, the blonde, racing frantically forward, tripped and sprawled over Anne's prone body.

"Bitch!" Sara gritted the word even as she struck the ground.

Anne gasped for breath, having lost a fair amount of it when Sara's body impacted hers. Then she was scrambling madly for an arm or a leg or a hunk of that long blond hair.

The two women twisted in primitive combat on

the rocky surface. Anne forgot everything she had
ever learned about ladylike behavior. She kicked and
shoved and lashed out blindly as the mist came and
went around them. Sara fought fiercely, but fortunately with no more trained skill than Anne.

Grabbing a fistful of the pale hair that was whip-
ping around in the struggle, Anne yanked violently as
Sara went for her opponent's eyes. Sara rolled aside
and Anne followed.

And then the bottom seemed to fall out of the
world. Anne felt the horrifying sensation of air where
hard rock should have been and realized that in their
struggles, she and Sara had rolled off the edge of the
cliff. There was no chance to grab for safety. It was all
gone in the wink of an eye. She could only pray that
the waves were coming in, not withdrawing.

Anne heard Sara's piercing scream as the two
women fell and then there was a jolting slam as the
chill seawater seemed to reach up to grab them both
out of the air. Anne managed to catch half a breath
before she went under. And then there was nothing
but shocking cold and stunning silence as the huge
roll of a wave gathered her into its maw.

JULIAN CAME AWAKE with a motionless, fully alert sensation he would have sworn he'd forgotten during the
past few months. Lying perfectly still, his head turned
into the pillow as he sprawled on his stomach, he
tried to identify whatever it was that had awakened
him.

Silence blanketed the house.

But it was not a normal silence. Instinctively he was
certain of that, and Julian had long ago learned to
trust his instincts. The old place was solid, built liter-
ally like a rock. It would not betray movement with
squeaky boards or hollow-sounding landings. Noise
could be heard if it was intentionally made. But some-

one was deliberately trying not to make any noise. He was as certain of that as he was of his bond with Anne. Both were gut-level realizations that did not need intellectual verification.

Someone was entering his bedroom from the hall. Someone who had a key to the old-fashioned door. He had jimmied Anne's door lock so that it could not be opened from the outside just as a precaution, but he had done nothing about his own. Partly out of curiosity, he supposed. You could get a lot of information about someone based on the simple observation of whether or not he'd go through a locked door.

Was it Hargraves or Craven, he wondered. And why tonight? Clearly the "foolproof" plan of Anne's had been far from *damn* foolproof. If he'd had time a few days ago he could have built in a few more precautions. But Anne hadn't given him time. She'd been set on carrying out the scheme on schedule. *When this is all over*, Julian thought, *I'm really going to lay down the law.*

At least he'd rigged the locks so that anyone trying to get to Anne had to go through his room.

It had to be Hargraves. Craven wouldn't be able to move that well. And there had been something about the light assured way Hargraves walked that told its own story. The real question, Julian decided, was how well he himself could still move.

No light had entered the bedroom when the door had been deftly opened, which meant that Hargraves had kept off the hall light. He would be working as much in the dark as Julian would be forced to work.

Another old, familiar sensation washed through Julian as he lay waiting. The tension of the hunt and the suspense of waiting to find out whether he was going to be hunter or prey released the cold awareness deep in his body. The energy hummed as the wait stretched out. Couldn't Hargraves feel it?

The soft rush, when it came, was not quite as professional as Julian had feared. Hargraves was good but he wasn't fantastic. Julian felt the launch of the attack the instant it started.

He twisted to one side, throwing himself off the edge of the bed even as something solid and very heavy landed where his head would have been on the pillow. Julian could see the shape of his attacker now, realized Hargraves was off balance as he put his whole body weight behind the blow. In that instant Julian knew he had him.

He came up off the carpet in a coordinated, spiraling motion that propelled him straight at Hargraves's midsection. The thudding impact as both men hit the floor managed to send a slight tremor even through the old, well-built house.

Julian didn't waste any time. His skills lay in his hands, and he used them efficiently. Hargraves recovered with surprising quickness, trying to throw off Julian's weight.

Both men rolled across the carpet, slamming into the wall. A small but heavy bronze of a rearing horse fell from the top of the bureau when Julian barely managed to avoid a chopping blow from Hargraves's fist. It struck the floor, missing Julian's head by inches.

The missed blow gave Julian the opening he needed. He aimed a short, crunching slice at Hargraves's chin and put all the strength he had behind it. Hargraves groaned once and went limp.

Julian gasped for breath, cursing the weakness of a body that hadn't been tested in many months. Lord, he was out of shape. He struggled to rise, aware of the pain from some of the blows Hargraves had landed. The other man's weight seemed exceptionally heavy as Julian rolled out from under the unconscious figure. Getting to his knees, Julian leaned down and put three fingers against the pulse in Hargraves's neck. The guy would live but he would be out for a while.

Glancing around the shadowed room, Julian remembered the lariat that had been hung as a decorative item on the wall. Stifling a grunt of pain as his bad leg protested the unexpected activity, he reached for the coiled rope and then turned back to tie his victim. He worked swiftly, thinking of his next move as he automatically checked the knots. He could take Anne out of the house by using her balcony-window exit. The keys to the car they had rented in Los Angeles were still in his pocket. Once free of the Creswell mansion he would make a few phone calls and get this mess straightened out.

And then he'd have a few words to say to Anne Silver.

But even as he made the dire threat in his head, Julian knew he was reacting to his own stupidity in allowing her to go through with the charade.

As if he'd had any choice.

The task of tying Hargraves completed, Julian got to his feet again, once more aware of the stab of protest in his thigh. Grimly he ignored it but as he reached for his jeans the bare toe of his already sore leg struck the bronze figure of the horse. Insult to injury, he thought savagely as he winced and swore very softly.

At this rate he was going to be forced to the conclusion that everyone and everything really was out to get him. He wouldn't be able to pretend he was merely suffering from a little paranoia. Bending down Julian scooped up the heavy bronze and then shoved his feet into the boots.

He still had the bronze in his left hand when he quietly opened the communicating door to Anne's room.

"Anne?" he whispered, reaching out to flip on the light.

"Not here, I'm afraid," Thomas Craven announced cheerily as the light came on to reveal his stout figure standing on the far side of the room. "For some entirely incomprehensible reason, Miss Silver saw fit to take a midnight walk along the cliffs tonight. No harm done. It was the direction we had in mind for her anyway. Sara has gone after her. Wouldn't want the little lady to have any unplanned accidents, would we?"

"You prefer the planned kind?" Julian stood quietly, his fingers still hovering over the light switch as though the sight of Craven's weapon had rendered him immobile.

"Ever so much more efficient," Craven nodded pleasantly.

"Except when things don't go quite right, as in Mike Silver's case."

"Yes, I'm afraid there was a slight mix-up in that instance. Either Mr. Silver's reflexes were better than Dan expected or poor Dan botched matters. He seems to be doing that lately," Craven went on musingly. He gestured significantly at the darkened interior of Julian's room. "I take it he didn't live up to expectations in there, either?"

"He's out of it for the duration."

Craven shook his head. "It's hard to get good help these days. Hargraves didn't even manage the simple task of seducing Miss Silver."

"That would not have been a simple task," Julian growled, aware of a new kind of anger ruffling his senses. Deliberately he tamped it down. Emotional reactions were guaranteed to bring disaster in situations such as this. He was experienced enough to know that. "I'm afraid that would have been an utterly impossible task."

"You must have made quite an impression on Miss Silver in a short period of time, then. Because according to our investigation she certainly is not engaged to you or anyone else."

"And that's why you thought Hargraves could try the seduction bit?"

"It was worth a try. Who are you, Julian Aries? Where do you fit into all this? Where did Miss Silver find you?"

"She tracked me down to my lair. At least I think that's how she sees it," Julian said softly. "As far as who I am, that's easy. I'm exactly who I said I was: the man who's going to marry her. Which is why Sara's seduction attempt wouldn't have worked on me any more than Hargraves's did on Anne."

For the first time since he'd met the man, Julian saw a flash of real emotion in Craven's expression. The emotion, interestingly enough, was fury.

"What seduction attempt? Sara was never assigned to seduce you, Aries!"

"Then what was she doing at my door the other night?" Julian inquired sardonically, recognizing that he'd finally hit a raw spot. About time. "Selling Girl Scout cookies? I haven't seen many Girl Scouts dressed in filmy little nightgowns—"

"You're lying! Sara is mine, she wouldn't dare—"

But Julian didn't wait to hear any more. This was as off balance as Craven was going to get. The other man's rage was the edge Julian needed. He hit the light switch with one hand, and as the room was plunged into temporary, blinding darkness he sent the heavy bronze horse hurtling toward the point where Craven had been standing.

The gun went off, whether by intention or out of a reflex action on Craven's part, Julian didn't know. In any event the shot went wide as a solid thud and a painful groan announced that the rearing horse had found its mark. Flicking the light switch back on, Julian leaped across the room, falling on Craven to finish the job. He had been right. The stout, middle-aged man could not move well at all. Craven was neatly unconscious in a few seconds.

Julian staggered back to his feet, telling himself that when this was all over he was going to con Anne into massaging his entire body. After all these months of inactivity he was really feeling the strain tonight.

Hurriedly he cast around for something with which to tie his newest victim and seized on the gossamer netting that hung down over the empty, rumpled bed. He yanked on it and the whole mass came into his hands. The silky stuff twisted very nicely into a tough strand of pliable rope. A couple of moments later, Craven was securely bound.

A fierce sense of urgency was pounding through Julian now. Anne was out there on the cliffs somewhere with Sara in her wake. Matters had deteriorated very rapidly.

Julian flung open the door of Anne's room, realizing that Craven would never have been able to enter so easily if Anne hadn't conveniently opened the door for him, herself. Another point to confront her with when this was all over, Julian decided as he headed down the staircase as quickly as he could. Each jolt of his injured leg as he broke into an awkward, off-balance run sent a message of pain throughout his nervous system. But the leg was performing after a fashion, and that's all he asked of it tonight.

He was about to head outside through the kitchen door when he remembered the flashlights housed in a nearby drawer. Not bothering to turn on the overhead light, he reached inside the drawer and grabbed the first one that he touched. It was bulky, sheathed in a rubbery plastic. It had to be one of the waterproof types, he thought briefly. The kind that would still work after a fisherman or a camper accidentally dropped it into a stream. Maybe it would even float.

Pulling open the door he glanced out into the darkness, trying to get his bearings. He scanned the swirling mists and saw a jagged ray of light sweeping through the air. It came to a rest, sending a dull unwinking gleam back toward the house. Another flashlight, Julian thought.

The pinpoint of light served as a guide as he made his way over the rough terrain toward the cliffs. The utter motionlessness of the other flashlight worried him. It looked as though it might have been dropped. Julian didn't dare switch on his own light for fear of making a target out of himself. There was a good chance that sweet little Sara was armed, and he had no doubts at all about her being dangerous.

He came closer to the cliff's edge, following the unwavering beam of the dropped flashlight, and then he realized that he could hear sounds of a struggle over the roar of the surf. He was in the process of flicking on his light when a sudden scream rent the air.

"Oh, my God, Anne!" he cried out in agony as his beam caught the two women going over the edge of the cliff. "Anne!"

He plunged to the edge of the rocks, sweeping the churning waves below with the heavy-duty flashlight. Shock and fear clutched at his guts. He'd never experienced such a devastating emotion in his life, not even when he'd thought he hadn't been going to make it out of the jungle. Nothing had ever been like this.

"Anne!" he yelled in helpless rage, as the beam of his flashlight revealed nothing in the waves. "Anne, don't you dare do this to me!"

And then he saw pale hair floating on a wave. Sara. If Sara survived this and Anne didn't he would probably kill the blonde. He knew it deep inside.

But a second later a face surfaced next to the floating blond hair. It was Anne. And the only reason

Sara's hair was floating on the waves was because Anne was struggling to keep the other woman's face above water.

"Anne, let her go. Just keep yourself afloat. Don't waste any energy on her." Julian yelled instructions as he kicked off his boots. "I'm coming to get you."

Clutching the waterproof flashlight in one hand, Julian launched himself into a dive calculated not to take him very deep. The shock of the cold, seething water was enough to knock the light from his powerful grip. But when he surfaced an instant later the floating flashlight was hammering against his shoulder, driven by the force of the wave.

"Julian! Over here!"

He twisted in the water, searching for Anne, his fingers closing once more over the flashlight. The heavy waves had a strong, surging action he realized but they were normal, not storm-driven. They could be handled if he kept his head.

The light fell on Anne's face, and Julian struck out in her direction.

11

ANNE FELT AS THOUGH she had swallowed a large chunk of ocean by the time she surfaced and found Sara floating limply nearby. Instinctively she had shoved at the other woman, trying to put distance between them. It was then that she realized the blonde was almost unconscious. She didn't know what made her grab Sara and attempt to keep her chin above water.

Coughing and sputtering as she adjusted herself to riding the swells of the waves, Anne looked up as the beam of a light flashed over her and she heard her name called out.

Relief and panic went through her simultaneously. But before she could decide which reaction to favor Julian was already launching himself into a shallow dive timed to coincide with the waves at their highest. He surfaced nearby.

"You pick some pretty dumb times to go for strolls along the beach, woman," he gritted as he swam over to her.

"You choose some odd occasions to go swimming," she tried to retort but her heartfelt relief at having him with her took the sardonic quality out of her words. "Oh, Julian, I'm so glad to see you. I was so worried. How did you know—"

"Later." His powerful hand caught her arm providing welcome support. "What are you hanging on to her for?" he demanded indicating the groggy Sara who was starting to stir and cough.

"I don't know. It seemed wrong to just let her go."

Julian took Sara's weight. "I'll handle her if you're too soft-hearted to leave her behind. We're going to have a job getting back on shore. We can't climb up that wall of rock in front of us, and the cove farther along is going to be too treacherous with the tide in. We'll have to try another direction."

"Julian, over there, at the tip of the cove," Anne gasped. She set off in that direction, absolutely certain of her sudden knowledge.

"Anne, wait!"

But she knew he was following, dragging the barely conscious Sara. Anne headed toward the jutting rock. The waves broke heavily on either side of it, but getting to the tip itself was comparatively simple. The worn angle of rock functioned like the prow of a ship, dividing the surging water smoothly. Anne was careful to stay in the smooth section of thrusting water and found her footing fairly quickly.

"In here, Julian." She turned to see him struggling upright in the water behind her, dragging Sara rather carelessly.

He stood knee-deep in the foaming water and played the light over the dark opening in the rock face. "What in hell...? It's a cave. How did you know it was here, Anne?"

"I'll explain later," she said, scrambling up into the dense darkness of the cave opening. "Here, hand me the flashlight and I'll help you get Sara up the side."

"The last thing we want to do is get trapped in that cave, Anne. The tide is still coming in. Water will be pouring into that opening in a few more minutes."

"No, it's safe. It opens out onto the beach on the other side of this cove."

"Are you sure?"

"I'm positive." No need to explain just now exactly why she was so positive, Anne told herself. Men could be stubborn at times and this was not a moment for excessive masculine stubbornness. She reached for the still-limp Sara.

"If you're positive you know there's another exit from this cave," Julian began with obvious reluctance.

"I am. And it will save us the long swim to a safe beach. Come on, Julian. That water is cold." And the last thing he needed was this kind of exposure, Anne thought anxiously. The threat of the fever seemed to be hovering over him in her mind. The water was cold and the damp night air was even colder. She had to get him to warmth and safety. Her own reserves were depleted drastically, and she didn't know where Julian was getting his energy.

Without further argument Julian lifted Sara into the cave and scrambled up the side after her. "Anne, this place could be a trap if you're wrong about the other opening."

"This way," she said, trying to drag Sara. The blonde groaned and twisted groggily.

"All right." Apparently having decided to risk trusting Anne's knowledge of the deep cave, Julian turned his attention back to the burden of Sara. "On your feet, Sara, or we'll leave you behind."

"No, I...." Sara sputtered, coughing up water. Her breathing, although ragged, was reasonably normal, however. She seemed dizzy, reaching out to the damp rock walls for support. And then she appeared to notice Julian. "Help me," she whispered in her soft, theatrical voice. "It's been a nightmare. You don't know what it's been like, having to work for that man. He's forced me to do the most awful things."

"I think you were right, Julian," Anne broke in, utterly disgusted with the woman's deliberate appeal to Julian. "Let's leave her behind."

"You can't do that. I heard you say the water would be coming in here," Sara protested distractedly, real

fear twisting her beautiful face as the flashlight lit it
briefly.

"Come on, then. I'm through carrying you," Julian
announced. "Let's go, Anne." He pushed Sara into
line behind Anne and then handed Anne the flashlight. "Here, you seem to be the guide. You'd better
know what you're doing, honey, or I'm going to be a
little short-tempered when this is all over."

"I'll bet."

Anne took the light and set off through the cave,
her footsteps never hesitating on the uneven, rocky
floor. She didn't like caves—hated the enclosed, claus-
trophobic sensation they gave her. Just as Carlota had
hated it. But she knew the exit was up ahead and that
it would open out onto high, dry beach.

Carlota had hurried through this tunnel, entering
the cave at low tide. On the far side she would find
her lover waiting. And in the soft, sandy mouth of the
cave they would make passionate love until the tide
began to return. Always the tide set the boundaries of
their lovemaking. Carlota had to be back before the
water entered the lower entrance of the cave.

Carlota hated the tides because they always seemed
to conspire against her passions.

"Anne?"

"It's okay, Julian, we're almost through. Just a few
more feet." Following the winding twists and turns of
the ancient, hollowed-out rock, Anne lost all sense of
direction. No wonder Julian was questioning her. But
it would be all right. She knew it.

And then she tripped over a heavy object lying on
the floor of the cave and went sprawling.

"Honey, are you all right? Stay put, Sara." Julian
came forward to retrieve the flashlight and help Anne
to her feet.

"Yes, yes, I'm okay. Julian, let me have the light.
Hurry," she whispered as a frantic feeling of excite-

ment tore through her. The answer and the ending were here in this cave. "Julian, look!"

He peered down at the heavy, carved box over which she had tripped. It wasn't a large object and it was half buried in dirt and debris. This section of the cave was surprisingly dry, testifying to the fact that the water seldom, if ever climbed this high into it.

"It's just an old box someone left behind."

"Carlota left it behind," Anne said grimly, going down on her knees to pry at the carved chest.

"Carlota! Are you crazy?" Sara demanded, reaching out to cling to Julian in support. "We've got to get out of this horrible cave. We might be going toward a dead end. We'll be trapped!"

"Shut up," Julian said with a total lack of interest. He shook off her pleading hand and focused the light on Anne's scrabbling fingers. "Anne, we've got to get out of here. Leave that for now. We can come back some other time."

"I've almost got it," she said, yanking the small chest free with a desperate tug. As it came loose from a century of debris, Anne felt the sighing satisfaction and gratitude that suddenly filled the cave. She stood up, dazed by the flood of Carlota's emotion. "Julian," she whispered, "Julian, she's free. Carlota's free. She's going now, I can sense it."

Julian's face was lined with concern in the pale light that reached his features as he held the flashlight. "Come on, honey. Let's go. Everything's all right now, but we've got to get out of here."

"Oh, stop talking to me as though I'd gone crazy," she grumbled, clutching the chest and starting toward the far end of the cave. "I'll explain it all to you later."

Wisely, Julian held his tongue, reaching out to clasp Sara firmly and haul her along as Anne's pace quickened.

"There, feel the wind? We're almost on the beach."

Anne stepped out of the cave mouth a moment later. Overhead the stars shone with unexpected brilliance. The swirling fog had almost completely dissipated.

"I'm so cold," Sara complained.

They were all cold. Anne's fears for Julian's health returned in full measure. "Julian, we can't go back to the house. Craven and Dan will be there."

"Yeah. But they aren't going to cause us any trouble. I left them neatly tied up in our bedrooms. Now all we have to do is find our way back." He glanced around, sweeping the beach with the flashlight. "We've come farther than I thought."

"You're going to be chilled to the bone," Anne worried.

"So are you. Let's get moving," he growled.

"But the fever—"

He shot her a ferocious glance that shut her up immediately. Without a word, Anne followed him as he dragged Sara across the beach. In the distance she could see the bulk of the Creswell house, still in darkness.

Sara had gone mute right after hearing that Craven and Hargraves had been neutralized. She went sullenly along in Julian's grip.

They reached the silent house a short time later, and Julian dispatched Anne upstairs for dry clothes and some blankets. When she returned with her load she found that he'd started a fire.

"Julian," she said very carefully, "Craven is lying on the floor of my room groaning."

"He'll live."

In the face of that kind of professional callousness Anne wasn't sure what to say. She and Sara undressed while Julian turned his back and unabashedly stripped off his own clothing. Modesty was not the order of the day, but then, no one felt like peeping, either, Anne decided ruefully. When they were finished Julian picked up the narrow leather belt Anne had been about to fasten around her middle and reached for Sara's wrists.

Anne watched uneasily as Julian methodically and rather brutally strapped Sara's hands behind her back. Then he carelessly thrust her down on the couch and tossed a blanket around her. The other woman glared at him but didn't offer a protest. It was Anne who felt obliged to say something.

"Julian, she's hardly going to cause trouble now."

He slanted her a level glance, the golden eyes gleaming with an unnerving brittleness. Anne caught her breath at the ruthlessness she saw there. Then she remembered what Sara had said about an Aries man making a dangerous opponent.

"She tried to kill you. Don't expect me to treat her like a princess. Sweet Sara is lucky to be alive and I think she knows it. Go get us something hot to drink, Anne. I've got to make a couple of phone calls."

Aries men make dangerous opponents. Anne took one look at the shuttered, ruthless expression on Julian's face and recalled that she had once thought he might not be a very nice man when he was "working."

"Talk about the understatement of the year," she muttered to herself as she scurried off to the kitchen. As she left the room Julian was already reaching for the phone.

Anne returned sometime later with a tray of cups and a jug of coffee. She felt better, but there still seemed to be a lingering chill in her body. The sea had been cold, and the shock of events had also taken its toll. Once more she worried about Julian's health, but one glance at his face as he finished his conversation on the phone was enough to convince her not to bring up the topic.

"Don't worry. All three of them will talk. I'll see to

it. Just set things up with the local cops, Steve, I'll take care of the rest. I know, I know." He paused, listening impatiently. "Steve, haven't I always tied things up for you in a nice, neat package? Well, this time is no different." Another pause. "Okay, I'll be waiting. And thanks, Steve." He hung up the phone and turned his head to meet Anne's questioning gaze. "Good. Coffee. I need it."

Anne handed him the cup and was about to hand one to Sara when she realized the other woman couldn't very well accept it with her wrists tied.

"Forget her. She'll survive without a cup of coffee," Julian said.

Sara glared at him but there was an element of fear in her expression. Anne realized the other woman was very uneasy around Julian now. Ignoring Julian's advice, Anne held a cup of hot coffee to Sara's lips and let her take a few sips.

Julian just shook his head. "You're too soft, Anne." He leaned back in a chair, sipping his own coffee and scowling thoughtfully into the fire. "The cops will be here shortly."

"Did you call them?"

"Yeah. I also called a guy I used to work with. He's in charge of coordinating some federal law-enforcement activities in this part of California. He's going to keep an eye on the situation and make sure nothing slips through the cracks." Julian slanted a cool glance at Sara. "But somehow I don't think anything will. Sara and her friends upstairs are going to tell all to the cops, aren't you, Sara?"

"Bastard," Sara swore, hunching into her blanket with obvious discomfort.

"Yeah. I've been told that on previous occasions." He set down the coffee cup and got to his feet, running a hand through his still-damp hair. "I guess I'd better go upstairs and make certain Craven and Hargraves understand just how much of a bastard I can be when the situation calls for it."

"Julian?" Anne lifted her head anxiously.

"Stay here and keep an eye on our sensitive." Julian turned and walked toward the stairs with a grim determination that told its own story. Anne knew his leg was bothering him and she knew equally well that he'd never admit it.

"Who the hell is he?" Sara gritted furiously as Anne tried to hold the coffee to her lips again.

"The man I love." Anne pushed the rim of the cup rather forcefully against Sara's sullen mouth.

When the car pulled into the circular drive a moment later, Anne got to her feet, telling herself it had to be the law. A quick trip, considering how isolated the Creswell house was, she thought, reaching for the doorknob.

"Prue! Good heavens. What are you doing here at this hour of the night?"

Prue raised her right hand and displayed a small, wicked-looking gun. She sighed regretfully. "I was very much afraid that Craven and the other two might foul up even a simple plan like the one I'd made for tonight. And since you're the one answering the door, I can only assume I was right." She motioned Anne back into the hall. "Where's Julian?"

"Busy," Anne shot back defiantly, trying to adjust to the latest twist in events.

"I see. Then we'll just have to wait for him, won't we?"

"Prue," Sara called harshly from the living room as she heard the other woman's voice. "In here!"

"Shut up, you idiot," Prue Gibson snarled as she pushed Anne ahead of her into the living room. Then she glanced at the blonde's bound hands. "My dear,

you make a splendid actress but you do have your
limitations in other fields, don't you? Where are
Thomas and Dan?"

"Upstairs. Aries is threatening them or something,"
Sara told her swiftly.

"Julian! It's Prue. She's got a gun," Anne yelled and
then tried to dodge as Prue swung the barrel of the
weapon toward the side of her head.

The gun caught Anne a glancing blow that sent her
sprawling against the coffee table. She flung out her
hand instinctively to catch herself and struck the dirt-
encrusted chest that had come from the cave. It went
flying onto the floor, the old rusted catch parting
easily. The chest fell open, and a necklace came free.

"Pick it up, you little bitch," Prue ordered roughly,
her eyes never leaving the heavy, ornate object that
was now draped over the edge of the box. *"Pick it up!"*

Anne moved hesitantly to obey. There was no
sound from upstairs and she wondered why Prue
wasn't paying attention to the silence; the older
woman knew Julian was up there. Why was she staring at the necklace as if fascinated, Anne wondered.

Prue wasn't the only one apparently captivated by
the jewels, which no longer gleamed in their intricately carved setting. Sara, too, seemed hypnotized by
the object.

"A fortune," Prue breathed. "It must be worth an
absolute fortune. Where did it come from?"

"The cave. She tripped over it when we went
through a cave on the beach." Sara bent forward,
studying the necklace.

It was an interesting necklace, Anne had to admit,
but she didn't see quite what there was about it to
enthrall Prue and Sara. Still, she wasn't about to question their apparent fascination. Cautiously she moved
toward the fallen chest, watching for an opening.

A shadow flickered at the corner of her eye and she

caught her breath. Julian was in the doorway. As quiet as a ghost he'd made his way downstairs. Perhaps he'd used the back stairs, Anne thought vaguely. She knew she must not give him away.

Prue was scarcely even bothering to aim the gun now, so hypnotized was she by the tangled necklace.

"My God, those are emeralds," Prue whispered almost passionately.

"And the setting is gold. So much gold," Sara said, echoing the intensity of the other woman.

Anne wondered how on earth they could tell what sort of gems or metal lay under the century-old dust and grime. She moved to obey Prue's orders, trusting that Julian would know how and when to make his move.

"Hurry," Prue said roughly. "Pick it up and hand it to me."

Anne's fingers closed around Carlota's necklace, and in that instant she knew Carlota had given it to her. It belonged to Anne. Passing on the necklace to another woman in love was Carlota's ticket to freedom.

"You can't have it," Anne said quietly, straightening with the necklace in her hand. Over Prue's shoulder she could see Julian moving silently forward. "It belongs to me now."

"Take it from her," Sara snapped, her eyes vivid with a strange hunger. "Get it, Prue. Get it and then untie me."

"Hand over the necklace," Prue ordered, reaching out to make a grab for it. The gun wavered dangerously.

Anne pulled back, nearly stumbling against the fireplace. The heat from the flames licked at her as she caught hold of the mantel but she clung to the necklace.

Julian's voice cut through the tension. Almost casually he reached out and yanked the gun from Prue's hand. "That's enough, Prue. I was wondering when you'd turn up."

His calm, dark voice seemed to break the spell that held Sara and Prue. Clearly startled, and looking rather dazed Prue swung around. "Aries!"

"Julian, she talked about being the one who'd set up the whole plan tonight," Anne told him, dancing quickly away from the hearth. The necklace was still clutched tightly in her fist.

"I was pretty certain she had to be involved. No one seemed at all worried earlier about getting rid of the 'housekeeper.' Given the fact that she could have tied these three to our mysterious 'accident,' I thought that seemed a bit strange. There's no husband in Santa Barbara, is there, Prue? How long have you worked this little psychic bit?"

"For years," Prue snapped. "And it always went perfectly until that damn Michael Silver started poking around, asking questions."

"Ummm. Did you always lay the groundwork for the various jobs by getting yourself hired on the domestic staff of whatever house was being set up?"

"I don't have to talk to you. I know my rights."

"Rights?" Julian looked politely curious. "Someone who organized an attempt to kill my woman doesn't get a whole lot of respect for her rights from me. I'm willing to let the law handle you if it can. If it can't—" he lifted one shoulder as if the rest were obvious "—then I'll take care of matters in my own way."

Something about the way he said it must have gotten to Prue and Sara. They stared at him, reading the endless threat that swirled in the depths of Julian's tawny-brown eyes. They were still staring at him, strangely mute, when the sheriff's car pulled into the circular driveway.

IT WAS A LONG TIME LATER before Anne finally got the hot shower she had been craving since her swim in the ocean. The deep-down chill hadn't quite gone away although she hadn't been terribly aware of it during the scene with the law-enforcement officers. Julian had handled everything with a dispatch and cool professionalism that Anne found both a relief and an annoyance. She realized that while he could be a tower of strength in this role, he was also more unapproachable than ever.

Julian had used the shower in the bedroom next to Anne's, the one Sara had used. Anne knew he had not invited himself to share her hot shower because he hadn't wanted her to see just how much his leg was aching. Or perhaps he hadn't wanted her to know just how exhausted he was.

She was almost out on her feet herself, Anne realized. Her hand moved to stifle a huge yawn as she finished toweling dry and reached for her flannel nightgown—absolutely exhausted and still vaguely cold. She brushed her hair and then stood in the middle of the bathroom trying to decide which door to open, her own or Julian's.

A lonely bed or a wounded lion. It was a heck of a choice.

But there was another factor to consider tonight. Julian might or might not need her but she definitely needed him. The decision made, she flung open the door to Julian's Western-style room and found it empty.

It took Anne a couple of seconds to realize that meant he might have gone to her room to wait for her. Maybe he needed her tonight as much as she needed him.

For some reason that thought brought as much tense emotion as any of the earlier events of the evening. Cautiously Anne went back into the bathroom and opened the door to her room. Julian was stretched out on the bed, his arms folded behind his head. His eyes went to Anne's face as she stood silhouetted in the doorway.

"You look tired, honey. Come to bed," he rasped softly.

She hesitated and then padded toward the round bed. "I am tired," Anne admitted. "It was all so strange, Julian. I've never been through anything like that in my life."

"I should hope not," he said on a dry chuckle, reaching for her as she folded back the sheet. "You weren't cut out for this kind of thing, sweetheart. I want your word of honor that you won't get us involved in any more situations like this one."

"I ought to call Lucy and tell her it's all over."

"In the morning. It's late here, and it's three hours later back in Boston. She can wait until tomorrow." He stroked a hand along her shoulder and down her arm.

With a soft sigh, Anne yielded willingly to the soothing touch, and her own fingers met no withdrawal as she began to knead the upper part of his injured thigh.

For a long while they lay wrapped in silence, each soothing and relaxing the other. Anne nestled against Julian's bare chest as he worked his hand down her spine. He lay unprotesting as she continued the gentle massage of his leg with her free hand.

The mutual stroking and comforting grew from tentative to assured as the minutes passed, and finally Julian simply wrapped his arms around Anne and held her tightly against the length of his body. She rested her head in the crook of his shoulder and accepted the peace.

"Julian?" she ventured at last.

"Hmmm?"

"I'll never be able to tell another soul and I'm sure you'll laugh at me when I tell you, but I've got to talk about it just once."

"About what, Anne?"

"Julian, I didn't know that cave even existed until I found myself swimming toward it. I had no way of knowing there was an opening on the far side. I went down to the sea tonight in the first place because I had to search for something. It was for Carlota's sake. Julian, I think I've seen her ghost a couple of times since we've been staying here. I . . . I went down to the beach because she wanted me to go down. She wanted me to find that necklace so that she would be free. And . . . and she was dressed in riding clothes, not a fancy lacy gown, because she was planning on running away with her lover that last night. The necklace was hers. Her mother had given it to her. It was all she took the night she decided to run off. It was to help finance the escape with her lover, I suppose. Both of them knew they'd be cut off from their families."

"Anne, honey . . . ."

Anne twisted. "Please let me finish, Julian. I know it sounds crazy but I promise you that once I've told you I'll never bring it up again. I just have to get the whole thing out of my system. At any rate there isn't much more to tell. Carlota's husband followed her that last night and found her in the cave with her lover. In his fury he attacked her, and the man Carlota was in love with ran off like the coward he was. The chest containing the necklace was left behind, and no one realized it was missing. But somehow Carlota's spirit was bound to that necklace. She couldn't be free until the necklace was retrieved. She needed someone who understood and sympathized. Someone who would follow her to the cave and find the necklace."

There was silence from Julian. Anne shifted uncomfortably. "I'm sorry," she went on, embarrassed. "I know it sounds outrageous, and I know you probably think it's all a product of my imagination. I swear, I'll never talk about it again. I just had to tell someone once."

"Anne, honey, how can I laugh at your ghost story when I've got my own to tell?"

Anne held her breath, aware of a barrier crumbling—a barrier that had stood solid all these months since she had last seen Julian Aries. Afraid to move for fear of shattering the moment, she lay very still.

"I had plenty of visits from a ghost lady," Julian began slowly, his fingers threading through her russet hair. His chin rested on her head as he talked. "You were my ghost, Anne, and there were times when I thought that a ghost was all I'd ever have of you. That plus a few memories of you yelling at me for risking Mike's neck."

"Oh, Julian," she said sighing.

"I went back after bringing Mike to you. I had to go back. I had a job to finish, Anne. Too many people were counting on me. The twenty-four hours it took to fly Mike to you and return to the island were all I could spare. I shouldn't even have wasted that much time. But I couldn't just send him home alone. I knew you were going to hate me, but I had to face you." Julian moved restlessly and then went on. "At any rate I went back to finish the assignment and told myself, just as I had told you, that when it was over I'd return to straighten everything out between you and me. I had decided that would be my last job for the department. I wanted out. Other things in life had suddenly become much more important."

"Were you really going to come back for me?" Anne asked wistfully.

"Oh, yes. I knew that much. What was scaring the daylights out of me was the realization that I had very little to offer you. We seemed worlds apart in many ways. I didn't know how I was going to go about convincing you to give me a chance. Then everything about the assignment I was working on fell apart. There was a leak. To make a long story short, I was captured by members of the group I was supposed to be investigating."

"Captured!"

"Don't look so shocked. It was probably bound to happen sooner or later. I'd been playing with fire for a long time. I suppose it was inevitable that my luck would run out."

"What happened?" Her eyes wide with pain, Anne moved back a few inches to search his face. "You were hurt," she went on, answering her own question. "Those bastards hurt you."

His mouth crooked wryly. "It's nice to know you're on my side. For a while there I thought the whole world was working against me. I got hurt when I managed to escape. They had plans for me, I was told. They wanted information and they wanted to make an example out of me. Either way I probably wasn't slated to survive captivity, so I made a try for the jungle one morning when the guard took me out of my cage."

"Oh, God, they kept you in a cage?"

"I'd used a broken piece of glass from a bottle that I'd found to cut the ropes on my hands and feet. When the guard came for me he wasn't expecting me to be quite so, uh, mobile. I took him by surprise. Then I ran for it. Straight into the jungle. But the guard got off a few shots and one caught me in the leg. I managed to get into the safety of the jungle and promptly blundered into a member of the group who was returning to the camp. In the process of coping with him, I got a little cut up." Julian absently massaged the scar on his jaw.

Anne sucked in her breath but she said nothing. A primitive anger was rising in her, however. Anger against an unseen foe who had done such things to the man she loved. Given half a chance she would willingly have tried to avenge him.

"By the time I got my leg to stop bleeding and had time to realize I was completely lost in that damn jungle, I was not in the best of moods or the best of shape," Julian went on. "The wounds got infected over the next couple of days and I started getting feverish. I'd wander for hours telling myself that I was following the direction of the setting sun and then I'd come to and realize I had just been moving blindly through the jungle. Half the time I couldn't even see the sun because the foliage was so thick. And throughout the whole mess you'd see fit to appear occasionally. And that's when I knew I was really in trouble."

"Did you hate me so much, then?" Anne asked sadly.

Julian shook his head. "I never hated you Anne. But during my lucid moments I realized you were thousands of miles away. I developed a pattern. Whenever I could see your ghost I'd know I was hallucinating. When I found myself alone I knew I was in my right mind, muddled though it was. I eventually stayed clearheaded long enough to find my way through the jungle to the ocean and from there I could follow the beach until I came to civilization. Three days after I got back to the States I came down with the first bout of fever."

"And you had your hands full trying to recover," Anne said gently, running soft fingers down the hard line of his cheek.

"The doctors didn't know what it was at first and finally diagnosed a malarialike bug. They hope that the bouts will get less frequent and less severe over

time, but they also don't know how many more there
will be. Between that diagnosis and my wounds I
knew I couldn't go back to work for a long time, I also
knew I couldn't go after you."

"I understand, Julian. I think you were arrogantly
proud, hopelessly macho and downright wrong in
making that decision, but I understand."

"Honey, I wanted to come back to you as strong
and healthy as I had been when I left. I was afraid the
only reaction I'd get from you in my present condition was pity, and I also thought you'd still be furious
with me for getting Mike shot."

"Julian, the reason I screamed so much abuse at
you that night in the hospital was because I didn't
want you to go back to that horrible island, and I also
knew that nothing I could say or do would keep you
from going."

He looked down at her. "Is that really why you
were so upset that night?"

"Yes."

He groaned and pulled her close once more. "It's
been a long six months, Anne."

"I know," she agreed simply.

"I have even less to offer you now than I did six
months ago. Hell, I don't even have a job."

She smiled mistily. "Julian, you idiot, you don't
know it yet but you have a lot more to offer now than
you did then." *Now he could offer himself.*

He wanted to ask her what she meant but her soft
fingertips were brushing the hair back off his forehead, and her leg was lying between his thighs. The
flannel nightgown was a soft covering for an even
softer body, and Julian's head was beginning to spin
with desire. And he suddenly realized he wasn't feeling nearly as tired as he had earlier. Even his leg
wasn't aching so much.

"Anne?"

"Yes, Julian?"

"Is your ghost lady gone?"

"Forever. I thought she had left while we were in that cave but she hadn't. Not completely. There was something of her spirit still clinging to that necklace when the box fell open. Something that managed to hypnotize Prue and Sara long enough for you to disarm Prue. At least, that's the feeling I had. But now Carlota is really gone."

"And my ghost lady has turned out to be quite real." Julian bent his head and kissed her with an odd gentleness.

Anne forgot Carlota and reached up to twine her arms around Julian's neck. He might not yet be ready to hear her verbal declaration of love, but she had no qualms about making it with her body. She needed him tonight—needed his warmth and strength, and he needed her.

Whether he knew it or not, he needed her.

The gentle understanding that had been borne between them metamorphised into the desire that had always existed between them. The result was a limitless passion that swept through both lovers. Anne could feel the singing heat in her veins and knew it was echoed in the pulsing sensuality that caused Julian to shudder heavily when she touched him.

They moved freely together, touching, coaxing, demanding responses. Their bodies twined and flowed, hardness against softness, dampness against heat, strength against gentleness.

Julian's hands caressed with wonder and need. When he traced erotic little designs on the inside of her thigh Anne caught her breath and arched against him with sweet abandon. She knew he gloried in her response. When she returned the caress, cupping the rigid shaft between his legs he responded in kind, thrusting himself more deeply into her gentle grasp.

The power and energy of their lovemaking both exulted and drained them. The fear and danger brought about by the events of the night faded as Anne was warmed by her lover's touch. Together they explored the farthest reaches of sensual comfort and sensual need.

Again and again Anne found herself at the brink of an incandescent excitement elicited by Julian's dancing, probing, thrilling caresses. Each time he felt her hovering at the edge he pushed her gently over until she thought she would go out of her mind.

Desperately she sought to take him with her, her tongue skipping lightly down his chest as her nails sank ever so carefully into the blunt tip of his manhood.

"I can't hold out any longer if you insist on playing with fire like that," he warned thickly as he moved at last to cover her.

"I want you with me this time," she gasped as he entered her, and he swallowed the sound of her words with hungry lips.

Then they were spinning through darkness and light, bound by passion in a manner that paralleled the way they had been bound together in danger. One kind of bond reinforced the other. In the end Anne could not imagine ever being free, or ever wishing to be free of this man again.

12

THE PHONE CALL TO LUCY AND MIKE wound up being held in an astonishingly loud tone of voice. The irate noise level was mostly from Michael Silver's end when he discovered that his sister and his fiancée had decided to go through with his original plan without telling him.

"How could we tell you, Michael?" Anne finally exclaimed in exasperation. "You had your hands full concentrating on getting well. We didn't want to bother you."

"Didn't want to bother me!" he exploded from his hospital bed. "I don't believe this. You went through with this thing without letting me know what was going on because you didn't want to *bother* me? Didn't you realize that the fact that someone had tried to run me down meant everything had drastically changed? Yet the two of you decide to just blithely go along as if nothing new had happened. As if everything could proceed normally. When I think of you out there alone in the Creswell house surrounded by that pack of wolves—"

"I wasn't alone, Michael," Anne snapped. Vaguely she was aware that she ought to be grateful her brother was feeling well enough to engage in the tirade. On the other hand she didn't envy poor Lucy having to take the brunt of his anger.

"You weren't alone?" he mocked. "Who the hell was with you? The ghost?"

"Well, I did have her help," Anne replied on a sudden note of humor. "But the one who saved the whole situation was Julian."

There was a beat of silence on the other end of the line. At last Michael said quite carefully, "Julian Aries? I thought he was holed up somewhere in the Colorado mountains."

"He was." Anne smiled, glancing across the breakfast table at the man in question, who was calmly eating breakfast. "I went and dragged him out and put him to work."

"You mean Aries was with you during this whole farce? Why didn't you say so?"

"You didn't give me much of a chance. Here, want to talk to him? I'm tired of having you yell at me." Anne handed the phone over to Julian who accepted it blandly.

"Hello, Mike. How are you doing? Good." There was a pause during which Julian's eyes met Anne's and his expression turned sardonic. "Well, I'm glad you're relieved to know I was here with her. Frankly, I had a few moments of extreme doubt, myself. But when I realized I couldn't stop her, there didn't seem to be any alternative to going along and keeping an eye on her." Another pause. "Yeah, it's all tied up. Prue Gibson was the real brains behind the plan. She'd set up a deal by getting a job on the household domestic staff whenever possible so that there would always be an inside person. Craven was the art expert and he took care of earmarking the valuables that were later to be stolen. Sara what's-her-name played the psychic and the guy named Hargraves was the muscle man. He was also the lock-and-key expert. He took care of determining how to get past whatever security measures were in place."

Julian helped himself to another slice of toast while Michael talked for a few minutes, then he agreed with something Anne's brother said. "I know. In this case it would have been child's play to get past these old locks." He took a deep breath. "I was thinking of asking Miss Creswell if she'd like an expert evaluation of her security system before I leave. She's got a lot of valuables to protect." He waited a little tensely while Michael said something on the other end of the line, and then he smiled with a trace of relieved satisfaction. "You do? Maybe I'll give her a call, then. Okay, okay, I will definitely give her a call. Thanks, Mike. What's that? Yeah. Something of a career crisis all right. Anne tells me it's all for the best, though."

He talked a few minutes longer and then dropped the phone into the cradle. Julian gave Anne a quiet, steady look. "Your brother thinks Miss Creswell would jump at the chance to have a real expert go through the house and update the security."

"Of course she will," Anne agreed blithely. "So will a lot of other people who have treasures to protect. Your background, disreputable as I happen to think it is, is just the sort to give people a lot of confidence in your security skills."

"It will be a while before the business builds itself into anything resembling a full-time career," he warned slowly, still watching her intently.

"About a year, I would imagine," Anne speculated cheerfully, munching toast.

Julian picked up his coffee cup, gripping it quite fiercely as he said in a suspiciously even tone of voice, "It will be at least that long before I'll be able to offer you much of anything. Anne, if I've made it in my new field a year from now, would you consider marrying me?"

Anne smiled very brilliantly, feeling her pulse pick up with happiness and excitement. "No."

Julian's face went very taut and the golden eyes pinned her. "No?" he repeated carefully. A strange mixture of emotions seemed to be passing through those tawny eyes. Anne read everything from pain to fear and anger.

"No," she said quite steadily, "I will not wait an entire year to marry you. I figure we can stop off in Las Vegas on our way back East to see my brother. No waiting period in Nevada. We'll be married by the time we reach Boston." She poured more coffee while Julian continued to sit staring at her.

"You'll marry me right away?"

"Julian," she admonished with mock severity, "you should have been proposing to me six months ago. I've waited long enough to wring an offer of marriage out of you. I'm not going to wait another year."

"Anne, are you sure?" he pressed roughly. "I have nothing to offer you now."

"You're wrong, you know," she said gently. "Now you can offer me yourself. Six months ago you were as hard and as self-contained as a chunk of granite." Anne paused to slant him a wicked little grin. "Sexy as hell, mind you, but still not quite human."

"You think I'm more human now?" he growled.

"Ummm," she said nodding. "You're still arrogant and proud and capable of annoying me no end but you're very, very human. You're also everything a woman could want in a husband: strong, protective and passionate."

A strange smile curved his mouth. "That's funny. I was going to say something similar to you. You're everything a man could want in a wife: strong, protective and passionate. And you can cook."

"I don't do windows," she warned.

"Anne, I love you."

Anne choked on her coffee, certain she hadn't heard correctly. Sputtering and coughing, she managed to squeak, "What?"

He frowned. "You heard me."

"How long...how long have you known?"

His frown deepened thoughtfully. And then he shrugged. "I don't know. Maybe I realized it on some level when I kept hallucinating about you in the jungle. I suppose I knew it for certain after those three days in the cabin. Until that point I knew I wanted you, but after that I began to realize that I—" He broke off quite abruptly on a sneeze.

Anne stared at him. "Julian?"

He sneezed again, using a paper napkin as a tissue. "Oh, hell."

Anne stood up and came around the table. "Are you feeling all right?"

"As a matter of fact, no." He sounded grimly furious.

"Actually, I've been feeling a bit off myself this morning. My throat's a little scratchy," she admitted. She put her hand on his forehead. "Hmmm."

"Anne, if it's that fever again, I swear, I'll...." The sentence trailed off in frustration as Julian blew his nose.

"It's not the fever," Anne told him calmly.

He looked up at her over the cloud of napkin he was holding to his nose. "You don't think so?" There was a flare of desperate hope in his gaze.

She swallowed experimentally, feeling the slightly dry sensation in her throat. "Julian, I have a feeling you and I are about to experience a rather unique brand of togetherness. We're going to have to share an old-fashioned cold. Come on. Let's get a fire built. I'll make a large pot of hot tea with lemon, and we can sit in front of the fireplace and comfort each other."

"It's probably from that dip in the ocean last night," Julian offered, looking a great deal more cheerful than he had a moment ago.

"Possibly. Or perhaps one of those four turkey houseguests we've been entertaining was coming down with a cold and passed it along to us before we got rid of him or her. That Sara what's-her-name always looked a bit sickly to me."

An hour later, ensconced at opposite ends of the long sofa, their feet touching under a quilt, Julian toasted Anne with a mug of hot tea.

"Comfy?" he asked with a chuckle. He had a fire going and had placed a box of tissues at both ends of the couch.

"Perfectly," she murmured. "Julian, you never finished what you started to say earlier."

"About how I knew I loved you? I suppose I acknowledged that about the same time I realized I needed you." His face sobered. "I've never needed anyone before, Anne. It was a very strange sensation. And I've never really wanted anyone to need me. It made life simpler."

"And now?" she asked tremulously.

"And now I realize how much I want you to need me." He looked at her. "You love me, don't you?"

She didn't hesitate. "Yes."

He nodded in quiet satisfaction. "After I'd decided you weren't pitying me and after I realized that you could care for me one moment and come alive with passion the next, I knew that what you felt encompassed a lot more than physical attraction. Six months ago I thought the attraction was all we had on which to build—another reason why I didn't want you to see me while I was recovering."

"There was no need to worry," Anne told him dryly. "Even wounded and feverish you were quite capable of sweeping me off my feet!"

He grinned at that, masculine arrogance stamped plainly on his hard features. "Taking you to bed was the most therapeutic thing I'd done in six months, and you were going to deny it had even happened," he accused.

"I have my pride, too, you know," she reminded him gently.

"We both do. But it's not going to stand between us again, is it?" he asked very seriously.

"No. Julian," she whispered, her happiness brimming in her eyes, "I love you so much. I love you and need you and want you."

"Not any more than I love and need and want you." He set down his mug of tea, reached over to remove hers from her fingers and pulled her into the curve of his arm. "I'll take care of you, Anne."

"And I'll take care of you. It's all part of loving."

"No more ghosts?" he asked almost whimsically, ruffling her hair with his hand.

"No. How about you?"

"No more ghosts for me, either."

"I do have a question, however," she began deliberately.

"What's that?" He bent to drop a small kiss on the nape of her neck.

"You never did tell me exactly when your birthday is. Are you an Aries?"

He grinned—a slashing, piratical smile that caught at Anne's heart. "I'll tell you on our wedding night," he promised.

The Fourth
Harlequin American Romance
Premier Edition

GENTLY INTO NIGHT

KATHERINE COFFARO

Emily Ruska and Joel Kline
are two New York City police detectives
caught between conflicting values
and an undeniable attraction
for each other.

Exclusive Harlequin home subscriber benefits!

- SPECIAL LOW PRICES for home subscribers only
- CONVENIENCE of home delivery
- NO CHARGE for postage and handling
- FREE *Harlequin Romance Digest*®
- FREE BONUS books
- NEW TITLES 2 months ahead of retail
- MEMBER of the largest romance fiction book club in the world